"Katie, if more people were like you then the world would be a much better place, believe me."

He touched her lightly on the cheek then strode away. Katie bit her lip as she watched him hurrying to the stairs. He gave out such mixed signals that it was no wonder she felt confused. One minute he was pushing her away and the next.... Well, the next he was behaving as though he really *felt* something for her. Was it just that he was an inveterate flirt and couldn't help coming on to a woman: the gentle touch, the intimate smile, the lingering eye contact? Or was there more to it than that? Did Nick really feel something for *her*, perhaps?

Dear Reader,

Midwife Katie Denning never imagined that she would meet the man of her dreams while dressed as an elf! Desperate to find a replacement Santa for the hospital's Christmas carol concert, she accosts a tall, dark, handsome stranger in the car park and begs him for help. All she needs is someone who can be nice to the kids and do a bit of ho-ho-ho-ing and their new specialist registrar, Nick Lawson, seems to be perfect for her requirements.

Despite his misgivings, Nick agrees to help and proves to be a huge hit with the children. He certainly makes their wishes come true by turning himself into the perfect Santa, but can he make Katie's wish come true as well? All Katie wants is a man who will love her as much as she loves him, but Nick seems reluctant to make a commitment to her despite their shared attraction. Can she convince him that love can overcome any obstacle if that is what they both wish for?

I had enormous fun writing this book. Nick and Katie are both lovely characters and deserve to find happiness together. *The Midwife's New Year Wish* is the latest book in my Dalverston General Hospital series and I would like to thank you all for writing to tell me how much you have been enjoying it.

I hope you have a wonderful Christmas and New Year, and that all *your* wishes come true.

Jennifer

P.S. You can e-mail me at: jennifer@jennifer-taylor.com.

The Midwife's New Year Wish

Jennifer Taylor

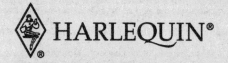

HARLEQUIN®

· TORONTO · NEW YORK · LONDON
AMSTERDAM · PARIS · SYDNEY · HAMBURG
STOCKHOLM · ATHENS · TOKYO · MILAN · MADRID
PRAGUE · WARSAW · BUDAPEST · AUCKLAND

ISBN 0-373-06486-1

THE MIDWIFE'S NEW YEAR WISH

First North American Publication 2004

www.eHarlequin.com

Printed in U.S.A.

CHAPTER ONE

'OK, FOLKS, can we have a bit of hush while I check that everyone's here?'

Katie Denning flicked the pompom attached to her bright green elf's cap out of her eyes and consulted her list. It was Christmas Eve and the staff at Dalverston General Hospital were about to perform their annual Christmas carol concert. It was the first time that Katie had organised the event and she was determined that it was going to be a huge success. She'd spent hours working on their costumes but it had been worth it, she decided, looking around the room. Never had she seen such a well-dressed collection of elves and fairies in her entire life!

'Right, if you could all shout out when I call your names it would be a big help,' she instructed. 'I'll start with the fairies so that's Anne, Vicky, Linda and Jane.'

'Here!' they chorused obediently.

Katie put ticks beside their names then worked her way down the list, ticking off the elves, the reindeer and George, the hospital's head porter, who'd agreed to be a snowman that year. 'So that just leaves Santa,' she concluded, glancing up and frowning when she realised that Jim Carstairs, the surgical registrar who'd offered to play Father Christmas, was nowhere in sight. 'Has anyone seen Jim today? I hope he hasn't gone off sick with that flu bug that's been doing the rounds.'

'He was in Theatre when I last saw him,' Vicky explained helpfully. 'He said to tell you that he'd be along as soon as he'd finished so I don't know what's happened to him.'

'I'll give Theatre a ring and find out,' Katie said, hurrying to the phone. She put through a call to Theatre, her heart sinking when one of the staff there explained there'd been a problem with the patient they'd been operating on and that she had no idea how long it would be now before Jim was free to leave.

Katie thanked her and hung up but it was going to cause no end of problems if she had to find a replacement for Jim so late in the day. They could always go ahead without him, of course, but the kids on the children's ward would be so disappointed if Santa didn't turn up for his promised visit and Katie hated to think of all their sad little faces. She quickly explained her predicament to the others, sighing when everyone groaned.

'I know. It's going to be almost impossible to find someone to take Jim's place at this stage. I daren't try and filch anyone else from the wards because we're already working on minimum staffing levels as it is.'

'How about one of the visitors?' Anne suggested. 'Visiting hour is just about to finish so if you're quick you might be able to waylay somebody suitable. I'm sure you'll find someone willing to play the part if you tell them it's for the benefit of the kids.'

'Good idea!' Katie exclaimed in relief. 'You lot stay here and I'll see who I can find. If I hang about by the main entrance surely I'll find someone willing to spare a couple of hours.'

'Just make sure that you don't scare the pants off them,' Pete Gilchrist, one of the paramedics, put in with a grin. 'It *is* Christmas Eve, don't forget, so a few of the visitors might have had a celebratory drink. You could give someone a very nasty turn if they see you loitering about in that get-up!'

'Cheek! I thought it looked rather fetching on me, too.'

Katie grinned as she smoothed the bright green tabard over her hips. With it she was wearing a pair of green and red striped tights and green felt slippers. She'd pinned her light brown hair under her cap and painted green and red freckles across the bridge of her nose so she could well imagine the shock she might give any unwary visitor who'd been imbibing a drop or two of Christmas cheer.

She rolled her eyes when everyone jeered. 'All right, I suppose we don't want to go *touting* for business so I promise I'll be careful. Back in a sec!'

She hurried out of the staffroom and made her way to the main entrance. There were a lot of visitors leaving and she smiled to herself when she saw the surprise on their faces as she hurried past. She spotted a couple of children staring at her and waggled her fingers at them, and they laughed and waved back. At least she didn't look too scary to *them*, Katie thought with a chuckle.

There was quite a crush in the foyer so she found a quiet spot near the coffee-machine from where she could check out everyone who was leaving. Jim was six feet tall so whoever wore the costume would need to be roughly the same height because there was no time to shorten it. It would also help if he was as comfortably rounded as Jim was, too, although she could probably find some padding at a push. Hair colour wasn't a problem because she'd managed to borrow a curly white wig from one of the patients on the oncology unit, and age also wasn't an issue because the thick white beard she'd fashioned out of cotton wool would hide a multitude of sins. No, all she needed was a healthy, six-foot-tall male, willing to help, and everything would be fine.

Knowing what she needed and finding it, however, proved to be two entirely separate issues. As the flow of visitors tailed off to a trickle, Katie started getting desperate. She'd not seen a single man who'd fit the bill the whole time she'd been standing there so now what was she going to do? She could hardly go out into the street and accost people…

Could she?

Katie didn't hesitate as she hurried outside. She didn't want to have second thoughts about the wisdom of what she was doing because there wasn't time. There had to be at least *one* eligible male in the town who could play Santa! She raced across the car park towards the main road then yelped in alarm when a car door suddenly opened directly in front of her. She managed to side-step the obstruction and ground to an ungainly halt as she glared at the hapless driver.

'Why don't you look what you're doing? You could have knocked me over just now!'

'I'm really sorry but I didn't see you.'

The voice was deep and tinged with amusement but Katie was in no mood to appreciate the joke. The concert was due to start in less than half an hour's time and her star performer was missing. She scowled at the man as he climbed unhurriedly out of his car. 'Then you should be more careful in future.'

'Oh, I shall. I'll make a point of checking for low-flying elves every time I park here from now on.'

This time he didn't attempt to hide his laughter and Katie's mouth pursed. 'And so you should. It could have been a child you almost flattened with that door.'

'It could indeed. Good job it was only an elf. I mean,

you're supposed to be immortal, aren't you, so no harm would have been done.' He smiled calmly at her as he took a bag out of the back of the car and locked the door.

Katie glowered back, not sure she enjoyed being the butt of his jokes. Normally she had a very good sense of humour but she was too stressed to appreciate his clever remarks at that moment. 'Oh, ha, ha, very funny. I'd split my sides laughing if I had the time to spare.'

'Thank you. I didn't realise that I could appeal to an elf's sense of humour as well as everyone else's. It's always good to know that you can spread a little happiness as you pass through this life, isn't it?'

With that he sketched her a wave and headed towards the hospital's main entrance. Katie glared after him, wishing she had the time to tell him exactly where he could get off… She blinked when it suddenly struck her what she was seeing.

Six feet tall.

Male.

Apparently fit and obviously not in a hurry if the way he was *sauntering* up the path was anything to go by. He fitted her requirements to a T and she wasn't about to let him slip through her fingers because he had a particularly irritating sense of humour!

She charged after him and grabbed hold of his arm so that he was forced to stop. 'What are you doing for the next hour?'

'Why? Are you thinking of initiating me into your elfin coven?'

'It's witches that have covens, not elves!' she retorted.

'Are you sure?' He tipped his head to the side and

regarded her thoughtfully. 'So what do elves have then? A brotherhood? A family? A—?'

'Oh, for pity's sake, I don't know!' Her fingers gripped his arm as she struggled to regain control of her normally even temper. 'I've no idea what elves do in their private lives. I'm really not interested! I just want to know if you can spare an hour to help give some sick kids a decent Christmas.'

'What exactly did you have in mind?' he asked with a marked lack of enthusiasm. However, Katie wasn't about to let that deter her.

'I need someone to play Santa at the Christmas carol concert. One of the surgical team was going to do it but he's stuck in Theatre and can't get away.'

'Surely there must be someone else who could take over from him.'

'You'd think so, wouldn't you?' She snorted in disgust. 'I mean, it's not asking much, is it? All I need is a man who's roughly six feet tall so he'll fit the costume and who's willing to smile at the kids and do a bit of ho-ho-hoing...' She stopped and stared at him. 'You can do all that, can't you?'

'Smile at the kids or go ho-ho-ho?'

'Both,' she snapped, because she really didn't appreciate all these wisecracks.

'I suppose I could manage it at a push. It all depends on the fee, of course.' He looked consideringly at her. 'What's the going rate for playing Santa these days?'

'You'd expect to be paid!' she exclaimed in dismay. 'But it's for the sake of the children.'

'No actor worth his salt would work for free,' he told her seriously. 'And that includes anyone playing Santa Claus at a Christmas carol concert.'

'But—'

'Tell you what, why don't we leave the subject of payment until later?' He grinned at her. 'You can judge me on my performance and then decide what you think I'm worth.'

'Well, I suppose it will be all right,' she conceded grudgingly, wondering where she was going to find the money to pay him. The costumes had cost a small fortune and she'd had to dip into her savings to pay for the material…

'That's settled, then. Let's shake on it.' He held out his hand. 'My name's Nick, by the way. Rather appropriate in the circumstances, isn't it?'

'I…um…Yes, I suppose it is.' Katie hastily shrugged aside her concerns about paying his fee because she really didn't have the time to worry about it right then. She took his hand and quickly shook it. 'I'm Katie Denning and I'm a midwife on the maternity unit.'

'Interesting job,' Nick observed lightly as he released her. 'So what do you want me to do? Didn't you mention something about a costume?'

'Oh, yes, of course.' Katie glanced at her watch and groaned when she saw how late it was. 'We'll have to get a move on, though. We're due at Women's Surgical in fifteen minutes.'

She bustled up the path, murmuring her thanks when Nick opened the door for her. She took him straight to the porter's lodge which had been turned into a makeshift dressing room that day and quickly unhooked the long red robes she'd made from the picture rail. Dalverston General had been built in the Victorian era—one of the many workhouse hospitals that had flourished in those days—and parts of the building still bore the evidence of its grim past. She saw Nick frown as he looked around the room and immediately guessed what he was thinking.

'The rest of the hospital is very modern,' she assured him. 'All the wards and theatres are in the new part of the building so it's just a few odd places, mainly to do with the admin side of things, that are still sited in the old section.'

'Thank heavens for that!' he exclaimed, tossing his bag onto a chair and shrugging off his heavy quilted jacket. 'I was just beginning to wonder what I'd let myself in for.'

Katie wasn't sure what he meant by that. However, a glance at the clock warned her that she didn't have the time to investigate it right then. She quickly took the robes off the hanger and handed them to him.

'These should fit you length-wise but you're a lot slimmer than Jim so I'm going to have to pad you out round the middle. Can you start getting ready while I see what I can find?'

'Will do.'

He obediently dragged his sweater over his head and Katie hastily averted her eyes when she was suddenly presented with the sight of a very tanned and very muscular abdomen. She quickly left the room, trying to blot out the image of that fit male body because she had more important things to worry about than her new Santa's superb physique.

Five minutes later she was on her way back with a couple of pillows and some bandages that she'd borrowed from the orthopaedic ward. There were just ten minutes left before the concert was due to start and she muttered a silent prayer that Nick would be dressed as she backed into the room. The timing of the concert was crucial if they weren't to disrupt the whole routine of the hospital. The day staff were due to go off duty at six o'clock when the night staff would take over. Several of the carol singers were on night duty, herself included, so it was vital that they finished on time. It was little wonder that her stomach was churning with nerves when she turned to see how Nick was faring, but she needn't have worried. Not only had he changed into the robes but he'd put on the wig *and* the beard as well. He looked so stupendous, in fact, that Katie gaped at him in amazement and he chuckled.

'So how do I look?' He performed a slow twirl, his hazel eyes gleaming with laughter as he turned to face her again. 'Think I'll pass muster with the kids?'

'Oh, definitely!' Katie could barely contain her delight. 'You look absolutely fantastic. You'd think those robes had been made specially for you, in fact. All you need now is the padding and you'll be the perfect Santa every child dreams about.'

'We aim to please.'

He swept her a laughing bow and her breath caught when she realised all of a sudden just how handsome he was. Even with that ridiculous beard there was no hiding the fact that he was an extremely good-looking man so that she was all fingers and thumbs as she set about fashioning a paunch for him.

'Here, let me help you. It's a bit tricky trying to do it all by yourself. If I hold the pillows in place you can just wrap those bandages around me.'

Nick quickly unbuttoned his robe and held the pillows against his tanned midriff. Katie took a steadying breath before she started to wind the bandage neatly around his waist. This wasn't the right moment to panic, she told herself sternly. She didn't have the time!

'You may need to fasten them on a bit higher up as

well.' Nick jiggled about, grimacing when the pillows immediately doubled over in the middle. 'See what I mean? Wrap some of that bandage round my chest as well. That should do the trick.'

Katie sucked in another breath as she set about bandaging the pillows to his upper torso. It was harder to reach around him now because he was so much broader around the chest and a spasm of awareness shot through her when her fingers encountered warm, bare flesh. It was a relief when the last bit of bandage had been fastened into place.

'That's better.' Nick buttoned up the robe, nodding his approval as he patted his newly acquired paunch. 'I look a bit more like the kind of Father Christmas the kids will be expecting, don't I?'

'You look great,' Katie muttered, quickly moving away. She'd fitted all the male members of staff for their costumes but not once had she felt as aware of them as she'd felt of Nick just now and it was rather alarming to have to admit it. She'd promised herself that she wouldn't rush into another relationship after what had happened with David. The next time she got involved with someone she would take her time and get to know him properly. Maybe there was an excuse for what she'd done because she'd been so lonely after her parents had died that she'd not been thinking clearly. However, she intended to learn from her mistake and not repeat it.

She cleared her throat, hoping that Nick couldn't tell how jittery she felt. 'You just need to put your hood on now and then you're ready.'

'Right.' Nick pulled the hood over his head then looked at her. 'How's that?'

'I'm not sure… I think your wig's a bit crooked.'

'Better?' he asked, quickly adjusting it.

'No, it's still not right. It looks as though it's drooping over your right eye.'

'You'd better do it, then.'

He sat down on a chair, obviously expecting her to adjust the wig to her own satisfaction. Katie went and stood in front of him, hoping he couldn't tell how loath she was to touch him in case the same thing happened again. Using the very tips of her fingers, she tweaked the wig into place then hastily stepped back when he reached for the mirror.

'That's better,' he declared, studying his reflection from various angles. 'What about the beard, though? It looks a bit uneven to me. Maybe you should fix that as well?'

'It's fine,' she assured him because she really couldn't face the thought of having to set to work on his beard next...

She bit her lip because she could just imagine how stressful it would be to smooth that cotton wool around his mouth. What on earth was the matter with her? she wondered desperately. Why was she having all these crazy thoughts about a stranger? It was impossible to say so it was a relief when Vicky poked her head round the door.

'How did you get on, Katie? Did you manage to find—? Oh, wow!'

Katie summoned a smile as Vicky came into the room. 'So what do you think of our new Santa?'

'Brilliant!' Vicky declared in obvious admiration. 'I don't know who you are in real life, Santa, but I'd let you bounce me on your knee *any* day of the week!'

'Thank you.' Nick grinned at her, his teeth gleaming whitely even through the snowy folds of his beard. 'I could return the compliment. In fact, the next time I need a fairy to assist me you'll be at the very top of my list!'

Katie quickly battened down her irritation when Vicky giggled. There was no point wishing that she'd been wearing one of the fairy costumes because that would be stupid. She headed for the door, deeming it wiser to stick to the task at hand. 'It's time to make a start so shall we go and find the others?'

Vicky hurriedly followed her out of the room. However, Katie couldn't help noticing that she hung back so she could walk with Nick. They passed a couple of late visitors who were leaving and she gritted her teeth when she heard Nick give a booming 'ho-ho-ho' as he wished them a merry Christmas. He seemed to be adapting to the role rather too easily, she thought sourly, then realised how perverse that thought was. The fact that Nick seemed to have a preference for fairies rather than elves wasn't a good enough reason to wish he'd make a hash of things!

The idea was so ridiculous that Katie chuckled then hurriedly turned it into a cough when she saw Nick staring at her. 'Bit of frog in the throat,' she explained, leading the way into the staffroom where the rest of the party was waiting. She quickly introduced Nick to everyone by telling them simply that he'd offered to play the part of Santa without going into detail. If he did demand payment then she'd have to work something out, but she wasn't going to spoil everyone's afternoon by mentioning money.

They went straight to Women's Surgical, where they were given a rousing welcome. Even the patients who were really ill seemed to cheer up as they worked their way through their repertoire of carols. Nick turned out to have a surprisingly good voice so that Katie was forced to admit that no matter what it might end up costing her, it could be worth it. He carried them through 'Once In Royal David's City' and took the lead in 'Silent Night', singing the lovely old carol with such feeling that there were several members of staff as well as patients with tears in their eyes when they left. It was the same in each ward they visited. However, it was in the children's ward where he really came into his own.

Katie was frankly amazed by his aplomb as they went from bed to bed so that Nick could wish each of the kids in turn a merry Christmas. He was a natural and she couldn't believe how lucky she'd been to find him, a sentiment echoed by several members of the group as they made their way back after the performance was over. It had been a resounding success and it had been all down to Nick for pulling it together.

Katie waited until they were back in the staffroom then clapped her hands and called for order. 'I just want to thank you all for today. It was brilliant and everyone loved it.'

She turned to Nick, who was surrounded by a group of admirers. 'The biggest thanks, though, must go to you, Nick. I don't think we could have found a better Santa!'

Everyone cheered and Nick grinned. 'It was my pleasure, although I'll be very glad to get out of this costume, I can tell you. Now all that's left for me to do is to claim my fee.'

Before Katie had time to realise what was happening, he stepped forward and swept her into his arms. 'I think a kiss should just about cover it.'

CHAPTER TWO

NICK had intended the kiss to be a bit of fun, a teasing reprimand because Katie had actually believed that he expected to be paid for playing Santa, so it was little wonder that he was unprepared when it turned out to be rather more than that.

He bit back a groan of delight as his lips settled onto hers. Katie's lips were so delicious that he felt like a kid who'd suddenly been let loose in a sweet shop. He could hear the others cheering him on but took no notice as he greedily savoured the taste of Katie's delectable mouth. Her lips were as smoothly addictive as caramel, as sweetly satisfying as barley sugar, and he just wanted to carry on kissing her and never stop...

'Oops! Sorry to break up the fun, but I need a word with Katie, if you don't mind.'

Nick was rudely jolted back to the present when someone tapped him on the shoulder. He let go of Katie so fast that she staggered, but there was nothing he could do about it. He moved aside so the other woman could speak to her, hoping that nobody could tell how shocked he felt. He'd kissed his fair share of women over the years, sometimes in fun although more often in passion, yet he couldn't recall a single kiss that had affected him the way that one had done.

'I... Is something wrong, Abbey?'

Nick's nerves twanged in alarm when he heard how breathless Katie sounded. He shot her a wary glance but she had her back to him now and he couldn't see her face. He sighed because even if she had been as moved by that kiss as he'd been, there wasn't a lot he could do about it. He'd set out his stall years ago and love, marriage and the regulation 2.3 children weren't on his agenda. Maybe he was making a lot of assumptions he wasn't qualified to make but something told him that Katie Denning was the sort of woman who'd expect all those things. A little light romance would never be enough for her. She'd want the whole kit and caboodle and Nick simply wasn't in the market for that kind of commitment when he still had so many dreams to fulfil. To put it bluntly, he wasn't the kind of man that Katie needed even if he'd have happily traded a few of his dreams for a couple more of her kisses!

'Did you page Niall? What did he say?'

The worry in Katie's voice cut through his thoughts and Nick frowned as he tuned into the conversation. Maybe he should have explained who he was earlier, he thought as he listened while the other woman—Abbey—explained that she'd been in touch with Niall Gillespie, the head of the obstetrics unit, but that Niall was stuck in traffic and didn't know how long it would be before he could get to the hospital.

Nick knew he'd been a tad economical with the truth when he'd introduced himself to Katie earlier, but he'd been loath to admit who he really was. He desperately needed some time to himself after the rigours of the past few months. That was the reason why he'd decided to move to Dalverston on Christmas Eve, in fact—because everyone would be too busy with their own affairs to notice him and he'd be spared any fuss. However, as he listened to the conversation, Nick realised that he might have to put his plans for a low-key Christmas on hold.

'Where's Julie gone?' Katie was asking now, so Nick held off a bit longer, hoping there might be another solution to the crisis apart from him revealing who he was.

'Julie went home sick at lunchtime. She looked really awful, too. I think she's got that horrible flu bug that's been going around.' Abbey sounded really worried. 'Karen Johnson's husband was frantic when he phoned to tell us that he'd had to call an ambulance. Apparently, Karen was in tremendous pain and losing a lot of blood. We didn't know what to do for the best when Niall told us how long it could take him to get here so that's why I came to find you.'

'You did exactly the right thing,' Katie assured her.

Nick felt a spasm of longing tiptoe its way down his spine when he heard the warmth in her voice. He could have done with some of her particular brand of TLC during the last few months, he thought wistfully, then quickly blanked out the thought because it was far too dangerous to go down that route. He forced himself to concentrate again as Katie began listing their options.

'Obviously, we don't know what's wrong with Karen yet but if it's a placental abruption, for instance, she's going to need surgery urgently.' She frowned as she considered the implications of that. 'In that case, bringing her here will only waste time if there's nobody available to operate. It might be best if she was taken straight to Hunter's Green. It will take the ambulance a lot longer to get there but I know they have an obs and gynae consultant on over Christmas because they faxed us a list of their staff in case of an emergency like this.'

'But they don't have a special care baby unit at Hunter's Green, do they?' Abbey put in anxiously.

'No, they don't,' Katie agreed. 'The baby would have

to be transferred to us after it's delivered and I can't say I'm happy about the idea of a preemie being driven around the country. Karen wasn't due till the end of January so the baby will need a lot of support at first. Damn! If only the new registrar had started before Christmas instead of after, then we wouldn't be in this mess!'

Nick sighed because it seemed that he really didn't have a choice any longer. He would have to come clean and admit who he was. He stepped forward, seeing the way Katie's grey eyes skittered to his face then just as quickly skittered away again. It was all he could do not to gnash his teeth when it was obvious that she was as sensitive about that kiss as he was. Now all he could do was to try and limit the amount of damage he'd caused, but he should never have put himself in this position in the first place.

'I'm sorry to butt in but I might be able to help,' he said with a smile that was meant to be cool but which wavered when Katie's eyes once again shot to his face and stayed there this time.

'Wh-what do you mean?' she stammered, and a shiver ran through him when he realised that he was responsible for that catch in her voice. The women he usually dated were far too sophisticated to betray their feelings that way, but Katie had no such pretensions. Nick found himself suddenly awash with tenderness and it was the last thing he needed when he was determined to behave in a purely professional manner from now on.

'That I'm Nicholas Lawson, your new specialist registrar. I should have introduced myself properly before, I suppose, but better late than never, as they say. Anyway, if I can swing it with Niall then I'd be happy to start right away instead of waiting until after Christmas.'

'*You're* the new registrar!'

A second or two earlier Nick had been glorying in Katie's lack of artifice. Now he found himself wishing that she'd made more of an effort to dissemble. Did she have to make it quite so clear how dismayed she was by the prospect of him being her new colleague? It was hard to hide his chagrin but Nick didn't have a choice.

'That's right. Sorry to spring it on you like this, but I've got references and everything so you don't have to take my word that I am who I claim to be. And, of course, Niall will vouch for me because he's the one who interviewed me for the post in the first place.' There was a hint of challenge in his voice because he really didn't appreciate the fact that Katie was staring at him as though he'd just sprouted an extra head.

'If Niall says it's OK for you to start then far be it from me to question his decision, Dr Lawson,' she stated coldly, then proceeded to ignore him as she turned to Abbey again. 'Take Dr Lawson to the office, please, Abbey. He'll need to speak to Niall and confirm that it's all right for him to start work earlier than planned. There shouldn't be a problem, but I expect Niall will want to make sure all the formalities are covered. I'll be along as soon as I've got changed.'

Nick just managed to step aside before Katie swept past him, not that she'd have had much hesitation in mowing him down, he thought. It was obvious that she was furious with him for not revealing his identity before now and he couldn't blame her in a way. She probably felt that he'd tricked her and that hadn't been his intention at all.

He sighed as he followed Abbey out of the room,

wishing that he'd never decided to drive up to
Dalverston that day. If he'd stayed in London over the
holiday then none of this would have happened. He
wouldn't have been pressganged into playing Santa and
he *certainly* wouldn't have ended up kissing Katie. This
seemed to be turning into a Christmas to remember.

Katie went straight to the maternity unit after she'd
changed into her uniform. It was a few minutes before
six and Jean Preston, the senior midwife on duty that
day, was delighted to see her.

'Oh, goodie! I was hoping the carol concert wouldn't
run on too long. How did it go? I was on the phone
when you came round so I didn't get much chance to
listen to you.'

'Fine. Everyone seemed to enjoy it, anyway,' Katie
told her briefly because she didn't want to go into detail.
The thought of having to explain Nick Lawson's part
in the proceedings was a little too much to swallow at
the moment. She would have to deal with the way he'd
tricked her, of course, but she needed a breathing space
first and swiftly changed the subject. She glanced at the
whiteboard where all the patients' names were listed
and nodded when she saw there was just one mum in
the delivery suites.

'Any problems there?' she asked, turning to Jean
again.

'No, textbook delivery from the look of it. She's one
of Anita's mums so she's only booked in for the birth.
She'll be going home after the baby's delivered so you
don't need to worry on that score.' Jean sighed. 'It
doesn't sound too promising for poor Karen Johnson,
though, does it? What a rotten thing to happen and especially at Christmas. Mind you, it was lucky the new

registrar happened to be here. It could be ages before Niall arrives if the traffic is really bad.'

'It was fortunate he happened to be around,' Katie agreed neutrally, although there was a lot she could have said if she'd had a mind to.

She picked up the pen and wrote Karen's name on the board in readiness for her arrival, thinking back over what had happened. Nick Lawson had never so much as *hinted* that he was a doctor let alone admitted that he was their new registrar. He'd had ample time to do so, too, especially after she'd told him that she was a midwife. Had he decided to keep quiet about his identity so he could make a fool of her perhaps?

Katie's pretty mouth compressed because she couldn't come up with a better explanation and it stung to know that she'd been duped. She should have learned her lesson after her experiences with David, but once again she'd been taken in. Nick had even led her to believe that he expected payment for playing Santa but he'd had no more intention of asking for money than she had of...of...flying to the moon and it was the fact that he'd set out to make a fool of her that hurt the most.

Anyone else would have explained who they were as soon as she'd accosted them in the car park, but Dr Clever-Clogs Lawson had been too busy having fun at her expense. He probably wouldn't have admitted who he was even now if it hadn't been for this emergency, and the thought of him turning up after Christmas after the way he'd kissed her was more than she could bear. What made it so much worse was the fact that she'd actually *enjoyed* the kiss, even believed that it had meant something, when all it had been was a way to make fun of her. Well, she'd be on her guard in future because there was no way that Nick Lawson would get the chance to trick her a second time.

'Niall's given me the all-clear so it's all systems go by the look of it.'

Katie swung round when she heard Nick's voice and felt her heart give a traitorous little flutter when she saw him standing in the doorway. He'd changed out of the Santa outfit and was now wearing a regulation green scrub suit. Like most of the hospital clothing, it had been washed almost to death so that the thin fabric hid very little of his powerful body. Katie's ears began to buzz as her blood pressure whooshed several notches up the scale. Nick looked the epitome of every movie hero doctor ever created—tall, dark, handsome, his brooding good looks enough to have the normally sensible Jean all aflutter as he introduced himself to her.

Katie, however, wasn't fool enough to be taken in by good looks a second time. She'd fallen for David *because* he'd been handsome and charming and it had taught her a valuable lesson. Appearance wasn't enough—it was what was underneath that mattered so the sooner she made it clear to Nick Lawson that she didn't intend to be charmed by him, the happier she would be. She was just about to set him straight, in fact, when the wail of a siren announced the arrival of the ambulance.

She hurried out of the office with Nick hard on her heels and went to open the front doors. The paramedics quickly unloaded Karen Johnson from the back of the ambulance and rushed her inside, rattling out information as they pushed the trolley towards the examination room.

'Patient's name is Karen Johnson, aged 32, and she's thirty-five weeks pregnant,' the young woman paramedic recited. 'Her husband told us that she's under your care so you should have her notes on file. She was conscious when we arrived but had lost a lot of blood so we've given her a litre of saline and have just set up a second.'

'Thanks.' Katie bent over the trolley. 'Hi, Karen, I didn't expect to see you here quite so soon.'

'I didn't expect to be here,' Karen murmured. She was obviously in a great deal of pain and that, allied to the massive blood loss, had left her very weak so Katie didn't waste any time as she pushed open the doors to the examination room and helped the paramedics roll the trolley inside.

'Let's get her onto the bed, stat!' Nick ordered, bringing up the rear. He put out a restraining hand when Karen's husband tried to follow them into the room. 'Can you wait outside, please, sir?'

'But I want to know what's happening,' Clive protested, trying to get past him. 'Why is she bleeding like that? Does it mean that she's going to lose the baby?'

'I'm sorry but we don't have the time for this right now,' Nick said firmly. 'Please, wait outside. I'll come and tell you what's happening as soon as I can.'

With that, he closed the door and walked straight over to the bed. Katie tried to hide her dismay as they quickly transferred Karen from the trolley because, in her opinion, Nick had been a bit rough on the poor man. She found herself mentally crossing her fingers that he wouldn't turn out to be a bit of bully like some of the obstetricians she'd worked with over the years. Her mums had a right to expect the kind of birth they wanted and she'd fight tooth and nail to make sure their wishes weren't ignored.

'Hi, Karen, I'm Nick Lawson, the new specialist registrar on the obstetric unit. It just so happens that you are my very first patient here in Dalverston so I'm going to make sure you get five-star treatment from here on.'

Katie frowned when she heard the teasing note in Nick's voice because it was a world away from the manner in which he'd treated Karen's husband. As she listened to him she quickly stripped off the blood-soaked sheet and set up the foetal monitor which would record the baby's heartbeat and the frequency of the mother's contractions.

'I want to examine you if that's OK?' he said, gently palpating Karen's swollen abdomen. 'Just yell out if it hurts or give me a good old thump if it makes you feel better.' He grinned at her. 'I'm tougher than I look!'

Katie was amazed when Karen gave a wobbly laugh. The poor soul was in a great deal of pain and terrified as well, but the gentle teasing had helped to reassure her. She stood to one side, ready to attach the monitor as soon as Nick had finished his examination. He was gentle but thorough, she noted, and she couldn't find any fault as he quickly established the baby's position before turning to her.

'Let's get a tracing of the baby's heart rate, please, Sister.'

'Yes, Dr Lawson.' Katie quickly strapped the ultrasound transmitter to Karen's tummy, glancing round when Nick said softly in her ear, 'Can you turn up the sound so Mum can hear that her baby's all right?'

Katie nodded as she set the dials so that a rhythmic beeping noise was emitted by the machine and she saw Karen's face crumple in relief.

'Oh, I can hear him! He's all right, isn't he? I thought he was…' She couldn't go on as tears overwhelmed her. Nick took hold of her hand and squeezed it.

'Your baby's fine, Karen. His heartbeat is a little faster than it should be because he's getting a bit distressed so I'm going to have to deliver him by Caesarean section. I know it wasn't what you'd planned but it's the best thing for both of you.'

'I don't care what you do so long as my baby is all right,' Karen gulped.

'We're going to do everything possible to make sure he's fine so you just hang on in there.'

One last squeeze of Karen's hand then Nick was all business as he turned to Katie. 'I want bloods for cross-matching and SCBU put on standby. They need to know that we have a pre-termer, thirty-five weeks gestation. I'd like you to assist me, Sister, so can you get someone in here while we scrub up? I've already spoken to the anaesthetist on duty and he should be here very shortly.'

'Of course.'

Katie went to the phone and called the nursing station to ask Abbey to take over from her. She checked the fluid and changed the bag then Larry Price, the duty anaesthetist, arrived, closely followed by Abbey. Nick had already left and she spotted him in the corridor as she went to get changed, talking to Clive Johnson. The man was obviously distraught at the thought of his wife having an operation and she sent up a quick prayer that Nick wouldn't be too brusque with him.

She pushed open the changing-room door then glanced back in time to see Nick slap the other man on the shoulder and for some reason her heart felt a bit lighter all of a sudden. Maybe it was silly but she was glad that her fears about him being a bully seemed to have been groundless.

Her lips snapped together as she let the door slam shut behind her. She wasn't going to go all soft because

Nick might not be the monster she'd imagined him to be. He would need to do an awful lot more than be nice to the patients and their husbands if he hoped to redeem himself in *her* eyes.

'Can you take him, please?'

Nick handed the squalling baby boy to Katie then turned his attention back to the child's mother as the infant was whisked away. Karen had lost an awful lot of blood and the sooner he got this sorted out the happier he'd be.

He swore under his breath as he carefully removed the placenta and placed it in a dish. Two thirds of the placenta had become detached from the wall of the womb and it was a miracle that Karen and her baby had survived the resulting blood loss and shock. Although placental abruption was fairly rare in the UK, it cost a lot of lives in developing countries where there was a lack of decent antenatal care. The condition was often linked to high blood pressure or pre-eclampsia, although there'd been no indication of either of those in this instance. He'd read Karen Johnson's case notes and there'd been no indication of anything wrong at her last check-up, two days previously.

Nick was suddenly filled with self-disgust when it struck him how close they'd come to a tragedy and all because he'd not wanted to tell anyone who he was. He'd put his own desire for some peace and quiet above the welfare of their patients and it was a salutary reminder of how an action could have far-reaching consequences. If he hadn't been so damned set on doing what he'd wanted to do all those years ago then his brother might never have died!

'Four pounds three ounces, with an Apgar score of six.'

Nick glanced around when Katie came over to tell him how the baby was faring. Thinking about Michael's accident always upset him so it was a relief to focus on something else instead. 'Not too bad a weight considering he's a month early. His score could be a lot worse, too. Are you going to take him down to SCBU now?'

'If you no longer need me.' She glanced at the patient and sighed. 'Poor Karen. She's had a really rough time. It must be even more of a shock for her because she had such an easy pregnancy. She didn't even suffer the odd bout of morning sickness like most of our mums do.'

'It's how it goes sometimes,' Nick replied flatly because he felt so bad about what had happened. If Karen had been sent to a hospital further away, her chances of surviving would have been greatly reduced. Time was of the essence in a situation like this so it was hard to keep the guilt out of his voice when he asked the anaesthetist for a BP reading. He saw Katie glance at him, as though she'd picked up on it.

A wash of heat ran up his face and he bent over the operating table because he really didn't want her asking him any questions and, after a moment, she moved away. Nick concentrated on the task of suturing as she left Theatre with the baby, stitching each layer of tissue with a skill and speed that came from long practice. Larry, his anaesthetist, whistled as he watched Nick put the last suture in place.

'I thought Niall was good but you're a real whiz with the old needle and thread. Good job my wife doesn't work here any longer or she'd be asking for your phone number. She's been on at me about having some new curtains made for our sitting-room.'

Nick laughed, appreciating both the joke and the moment of camaraderie. 'I'll have to send her an estimate for my services, although I have to warn you that I'm not cheap.'

'I'll bet you're not!' Larry chuckled. 'It must be a nice little sideline for you.'

They finished off soon afterwards and Nick thanked the rest of the team who'd assisted him. Although he'd been the major player, he couldn't have managed without Larry and the scrub nurse, not to mention Katie, of course. A buzz of heat sprang up in the pit of his stomach at the thought of Katie but he tamped it down as he went to get changed. Katie was a wonderful nurse and he must focus on that fact rather than any other of her assets from now on.

Clive Johnson was pacing the waiting room when Nick went back to the maternity unit so he didn't drag it out and add to the poor man's agony. He told him simply that Karen and the baby had come through the operation and there was a very good chance they would both recover from their ordeal. Naturally, Clive wanted to know what had happened so Nick explained how the placenta had detached itself from the wall of the womb and it had been that which had caused the massive bleeding.

He didn't expound on the seriousness of the situation because Clive wasn't up to it right then. However, he guessed there might be more questions later so he gave the man his phone number and told him to call him if he wanted to chat and left it at that. Abbey was in the corridor so he asked her to take Clive to SCBU to see his baby son.

Once that was done then, by rights, Nick knew he was free to leave but he was loath to take himself off in case anything else happened. Maybe he didn't *have* to stay but it would make him feel better so he went into the office and switched on the light. There was a kettle on top of the filing cabinet and it struck him all of a sudden how thirsty he was. He'd not had a drink since he'd arrived and a cup of coffee might just put a bit of fizz back into his veins and see him through the night.

He flicked the switch on the kettle then spooned coffee granules into a mug, added whitener and sugar—three large spoonfuls—and sank down onto the nearest chair. It had been quite a day, one way and another, and he was already bone tired from the long hours he'd been working recently. The kettle soon came to the boil and switched itself off but Nick never even noticed because he was fast asleep by then, his dreams full of babies crying and women with swollen bellies begging him for help...

Something green suddenly appeared just beyond his field of vision and his eyelids twitched. He could just make out a cap with a pompom, some pointy-toed boots and freckles—lots and lots of red and green freckles...

He sighed wistfully when a familiar little elfin figure suddenly materialised right in the middle of his dream. His life would be so much better if he had someone like Katie to share it with.

CHAPTER THREE

KATIE was on her way back to the delivery suite when she spotted a light on in the office. She sighed as she immediately changed course. They'd been inundated with memos recently about the need to save money by turning off lights and it was hardly setting a good example to leave one on in the office.

She glanced at her watch as she opened the door and frowned when she saw that it was almost two in the morning. She hadn't been into the office since Karen Johnson had been admitted so the light must have been burning for hours. They'd had three new admissions that night although, thankfully, none of them had presented with any problems. One mum had just delivered a healthy baby girl and was on her way to the ward, and the other two were well advanced with their labours. With a bit of luck both mums would have given birth before she went off duty so the day staff would have a clear run...

Katie stopped dead when she spotted the figure slumped in a chair. She'd thought Nick Lawson had left ages ago but obviously she'd been mistaken. Now she wasn't sure what to do, whether she should wake him or leave him to sleep, and before she could make up her mind, his eyes suddenly opened.

'Did you want me?' he muttered, dragging himself upright in the chair.

'No. I just came to switch off the light. I spotted it when I was passing and thought I must have left it on by mistake,' she replied hurriedly, wondering why she felt the need to explain how she happened to be there. Was it because Nick looked so appealing with his dark hair all rumpled and the shadow of a beard darkening his jaw?

She wanted to deny it but she was too honest to lie to herself. She might not *like* Nick for the way he'd tricked her but she couldn't deny that she responded to him, and it was hard to reconcile two such conflicting emotions after what had happened with David.

'Oh, I see.' He stood up then groaned as he began hopping up and down on one leg. 'Drat! I've got pins and needles in my foot.' He flopped back down onto the chair and removed his shoe so he could knead his toes. 'That'll teach me to fall asleep in the chair. I was only going to sit down while the kettle boiled but I must have dropped off.'

'You must have been tired,' Katie said lightly, hoping her confusion didn't show. 'Too many late nights, I expect.'

'Too many late nights on top of too many long days, you mean,' he replied rather cryptically. He slid his foot back into his shoe and gingerly stood up. 'That's better. Anyway, if I'm in your way just say the word and I'll find somewhere else to sit. I didn't mean to clutter up your office.'

'No, it's fine,' she assured him. 'Anyway, isn't it about time you went home?'

'I thought I'd hang on here in case you needed me.' He shrugged when she looked at him in surprise. 'I didn't want there to be a repeat of the Karen Johnson episode. If you're a registrar down because she's gone home sick then it could cause problems.'

'That's very good of you,' Katie said slowly, wondering if there was an ulterior motive to the offer. Maybe she was a little over-sensitive where Nick was concerned but how many people would offer to work on Christmas Eve if they didn't need to?

'There isn't a catch, if that's what you're thinking,' he said quietly. 'I just feel really bad about what happened earlier. I should have told you who I was from the outset instead of leaving it until we had a near tragedy on our hands.'

'But you weren't to know it would happen,' Katie protested, surprised that she should feel a need to defend his actions.

'Maybe not, but that doesn't alter the fact that Karen could have lost her baby and maybe even her life if she hadn't received the treatment she needed.' His deep voice was laced with guilt and Katie frowned because it certainly wasn't the response she would have expected from him.

'But she *did* receive the right treatment and it was all thanks to you, Nick. I don't know why you're blaming yourself. I mean, we weren't expecting you to start work until *after* Christmas so it was really fortunate that you happened to be here in the first place.'

'Maybe,' he conceded, although Katie could tell he wasn't convinced.

'There's no "maybe" about it. It was a stroke of luck that you turned up when you did. Let's face it, not many people decide to move house on Christmas Eve. They usually wait until after the holidays.'

'It just seemed like a good time to do it.' He went to the filing cabinet and switched on the kettle again. 'Everyone's always so busy at Christmas that I thought I'd have a couple of days to myself to get settled in before I had to start work.'

'I see. What about your family, though?' she asked curiously because it still seemed rather a strange thing to have done. 'Didn't you want to spend Christmas with them this year?'

'My parents got divorced a few years ago,' he explained, pouring boiling water into a mug. 'Mum emigrated to New Zealand to live with her sister and Dad remarried. He lives in Scotland now with his new wife and family.'

'Oh, dear.' Katie grimaced. 'That must be rather difficult—unless you take it in turns to visit them, of course.'

'No. Christmas is just another day so far as I'm concerned,' he said flatly, stirring the contents of the mug. 'I prefer to work over the holiday, but it just so happens that I was off this year because of starting this job.'

He glanced up and Katie shivered when she saw the bleakness in his eyes. She sensed there was a lot more that he wasn't telling her but before she could think of a way to ask him, he countered it with a question of his own. 'So what about you? D'you normally spend Christmas with your family?'

'No.' She summoned a smile but it was difficult to keep the ache out of her voice. If things had gone to plan then this year she would have spent the holiday with David, but after she'd found out how different their views on life were there'd been no chance of that happening. 'My parents died a couple of years ago in a coach crash. I was an only child and don't have any other family so that's why I volunteered to work over Christmas.'

'I see. Sorry. That was a bit tactless of me, wasn't it?'

'There's nothing to apologise for. You weren't to

know about my circumstances,' she said briskly because she certainly didn't want to be the recipient of his sympathy. Nick Lawson had aroused a lot of conflicting emotions inside her already and she didn't want to add any more so she swiftly changed the subject. 'Anyway, I'd better get a move on. We have two mums in labour so there's always something that needs doing.'

'Just give me a shout if you need me,' Nick told her, carrying the cup of coffee over to the desk and sitting down.

'I doubt we'll have another emergency tonight. Why don't you get off home once you've drunk that coffee? It seems pointless, you staying here when you could be tucked up in bed.'

'I'd rather stay in case anything happens.' He shrugged when she frowned. 'I'd just feel better about it so long as you don't mind. In any case, I'm not sure if I'll be able to get into the staff accommodation block at this hour of the morning. I should have collected the key to my room from the admin office when I arrived but I forgot all about it.'

'You're staying in the staff quarters?' Katie exclaimed.

'Uh-huh.' He took a sip of the drink then shrugged. 'I'm only going to be here for a few months so it didn't seem worth all the hassle of finding myself a place to live. Niall offered to get me a staff room so that will do me very nicely.'

'You'll find it very cramped,' she warned, knowing it wasn't just the shock of learning that a senior registrar had settled for the dubious delights of staff accommodation that disturbed her so much. The fact that she lived there as well was what she found really unsettling, for some reason.

'Is that where you live?' he asked curiously.

'Yes.' Katie summoned a smile because she didn't want him to suspect how uneasy she felt about the idea of them living under the same roof. It was completely ridiculous and she hurried on. 'It was only supposed to be a temporary measure to tide me over after I moved out of the flat I'd been sharing with my boyfriend, but six months later I'm still there.'

'Are you hoping for a reconciliation?' he asked, watching her over the rim of the mug.

'With David? No way! We weren't suited and I'm only surprised I didn't realise it sooner.' She cleared her throat because her relationship with David really wasn't the issue here. 'I just haven't had a chance to go flat hunting so it's been easier to stay put. However, living in staff accommodation wouldn't be my first choice. I prefer a bit more room to manoeuvre!'

'I don't imagine it will bother me all that much.' He grinned when he saw the scepticism on her face. 'You're talking to a guy who's just spent six months living in a tent so, believe me, it will feel like a palace compared to that.'

'A tent?' Katie repeated, forgetting her own concerns at this fresh revelation. 'What were you doing living in a tent for all that time?'

'I was working for one of the overseas aid agencies. You may have heard of it…Worlds Together?' He carried on when she nodded. 'We were setting up a new maternity unit in an area of India which has a particularly poor record of infant mortality and ended up living in tents because there wasn't any other accommodation available. What few resources the people have there are needed for themselves.'

'Sounds pretty grim,' she observed, watching him

closely so that she saw the shadow which crossed his face.

'It certainly wasn't a picnic.'

He didn't say anything else. However, Katie was left with the distinct impression that the experience had been a lot worse than he'd admitted. As she left the office, she found herself wondering if she'd been a bit hasty in her assessment of him. Was Nick *really* the trickster who'd set out to have fun at her expense, or was he a caring and dedicated doctor? Only time would tell but it was worrying to suddenly have these doubts about him.

The rest of the night flew past after that. Both mums had their babies and had been moved to the wards by the time the day staff came on duty. Katie handed over to Rosie Meadows, the young staff nurse who was in charge that day, and left her to it, yawning as she went to the staffroom for her bag. It was just gone six when she left the building and still dark, so she didn't linger as she walked the short distance from the main part of the hospital to the staff accommodation wing. She keyed the entry code into the security lock then glanced round when she heard footsteps and saw Nick hurrying up the path. He grinned as she held the door open for him.

'Thanks. You just saved me a journey. I forgot to ask the porter for the entry code,' he explained as he followed her into the foyer.

'Three-nine-seven-nine,' Katie told him helpfully.

'I'd better jot that down before I forget it.' He took a ballpoint pen out of his pocket and quickly wrote the numbers on the back of his hand. 'I'll need to unload my car later and it would help if I didn't have to go waking people up by ringing the doorbell.'

'You wouldn't be very popular if you did,' she agreed lightly, heading for the stairs. 'Most of the folk staying here at the moment are on nights and they'll be keen to get some sleep. Anyone who's off duty will have gone home to their families for Christmas.'

'Probably best not to get a reputation for being a pesky neighbour so early in the day,' he conceded as they reached the first landing.

Katie stopped when he hesitated. 'Which room are you in?'

'Number twenty-nine. Fortunately, the porters had a spare set of keys otherwise I'd have ended up sleeping in the residents' lounge. The admin office doesn't re-open until after Boxing Day, apparently.'

'Lucky for you,' she agreed, pointing towards the next flight of stairs. 'You're on the next floor, halfway along on the right. The doors are all numbered so you shouldn't have a problem finding your room.'

'Thanks.' He turned towards the stairs then suddenly stopped and looked back. 'Do you know if the staff canteen is open today? I meant to stock up on a few essentials after I'd got here but I never had the chance with one thing and another.'

'That's my fault,' Katie said guiltily. 'If I hadn't pressganged you into playing Santa you could have done your shopping.'

'It was just one of those things so don't worry about it. So long as I can get my daily fix of caffeine I'll survive, and I'm sure someone will lend me a teabag or a spoonful of coffee if I ask them nicely.'

'You'll need something a bit more substantial than coffee to keep you going!'

'Yes, Sister,' he replied with a grin that brought a rush of colour to her cheeks.

'Sorry. I must try to curb my bossy tendencies,' she murmured.

'Don't do so on my account, Katie. I like a woman who knows her own mind.'

Katie wasn't sure what to make of that and turned away, making a great production of finding her keys so he couldn't see how confused she felt. Nick had sounded as though he'd meant it as a compliment yet she was afraid to take it as such because she still didn't quite trust him. In the end she decided it would be best to ignore it and answer the question he'd asked her instead.

'The canteen is open today so there shouldn't be a problem about getting something to eat. They're serving a full Christmas dinner at one o'clock and a lot of the staff will be there. It might be a good way to introduce yourself to everyone.'

'Good idea. If I'm awake I'll go and join them.' He grimaced. 'Mind you, I could murder a cup of tea at the moment. I don't suppose I could beg a teabag and a drop of milk off you, could I? I don't think I can last out until lunchtime.'

'Of course you can! Better still, I've got a spare box of teabags and a jar of coffee in my room so they'll tide you over until you can get to the shops.'

'Oh, no, really, I can't take all your stuff,' he began, but Katie shook her head.

'Don't be silly. They're just sitting there so you may as well make use of them.' She briskly led the way to her room and unlocked the door. Nick followed her inside, glancing round as she switched on the lamp.

'Mmm, this is very cosy. And I mean *cosy* as in warm

and snug rather than as estate-agent talk for small and cramped.'

'Sounds as though you may have come a cropper when you've been flat hunting,' she observed, opening the cupboard and taking out the teabags and the jar of coffee.

'More times than I care to admit.' Nick propped himself against the doorjamb and grinned at her. 'I lived in London for a while and finding a place to live there was a nightmare. I've seen shoe boxes bigger than some of the "apartments" I viewed!'

'Is that why you decided to move north?' she asked curiously, handing him the tea and coffee.

'Not really. I was more interested in the fact that Dalverston has such a marvellous reputation. It's one of the top ten obstetric units in the country.'

'I suppose it's good to be able to put it on your CV,' she suggested, but Nick shrugged.

'That's less important than the experience I'll gain here.' He glanced at the items she'd given him, giving her no chance to question him further. 'Can I be really cheeky and ask if you can spare some sugar as well? I can drink my tea and coffee black but I can't bear to drink it without any sugar.'

'I don't take sugar but there should be some in the kitchen,' Katie told him.

She led the way from the room, wishing that she'd had the time to find out what he'd meant by that remark. In her experience, most registrars were more concerned about the prestige to be gained from working at Dalverston, and the positive effect it could have on their careers. However, Nick seemed less concerned with that aspect of the job than the experience it would afford him. She would have loved to delve deeper but there was no way she could think of to switch the conversation back so she found the sugar and poured some into a cup then took the spare carton of milk she'd bought out of the fridge and gave that to him as well.

'Is there anything else you need? Biscuits? Some bread? Maybe some eggs?'

'No, this is great. I'll be able to eat in the canteen so I've got everything I need right here, thanks. Obviously, I'll pay you back as soon as the shops are open again.'

'Don't worry about it,' she assured him. 'A few teabags aren't going to break the bank.'

'Maybe not, but I don't want you thinking I'm freeloading off you.'

'I don't. Really!'

'Good.' He grinned at her and Katie felt her heart give that odd little spasm again that it had done before and quickly turned away.

'I'd better get to bed,' she said, leading the way into the corridor. Maybe Nick did have an odd effect on her but it would be foolish to read too much into it when she was so tired.

Nick glanced at his watch as he followed her out of the kitchen and groaned. 'Is that really the time? You must be cursing me for keeping you chatting when you want to get to sleep. Thanks again, Katie. You're a real life-saver.'

With that he disappeared towards the stairs and Katie heard him walking along the upper landing as she made her way back to her room. She undressed and took a quick shower in the tiny *en suite* bathroom. Ten minutes later she was in bed but even though she was tired after the busy night she'd had, sleep was a long time coming. And when she did finally drift off she dreamt that Santa was kissing her…a Santa who looked remarkably like Nick Lawson, in fact.

The staff canteen was packed when Nick arrived shortly after one o'clock that afternoon. He joined the queue at the serving counter and opted for a full Christmas lunch when his turn came. He was ravenously hungry and the crisp roast potatoes, turkey and vegetables looked absolutely delicious.

He paid for his meal then looked for somewhere to sit, half hoping that he'd spot Katie and half hoping that he wouldn't. He knew it would be unfair to make a play for her but it didn't stop him enjoying being with her so it was rather a mixed blessing when he couldn't see any sign of her in the canteen. He finally opted for an empty seat at a table near the door and introduced himself to the rest of the people at the table as he sat down. One of the nurses worked on the children's ward and remembered him from the carol concert so that broke the ice. Nick soon found himself drawn into the conversation and was even starting to enjoy himself when the same nurse suddenly spotted a friend coming into the canteen and waved to her.

Nick obligingly moved up to make room for the newcomer but it was only when he saw Katie carrying her tray across the room that he realised she was going to join them. His heart gave a little leap of excitement as she squeezed into the gap beside him but he quickly battened it down. Katie wasn't the type of woman who fitted his usual requirements for a girlfriend, he reminded himself sternly, and he mustn't take the chance of hurting her… He almost choked on a sprout when he realised how arrogant that sounded when there was no reason to imagine that Katie was the least bit interested in him!

'I see you made it up in time for lunch,' she said lightly once she'd greeted the others. However, Nick was very aware that she had avoided meeting his eyes.

'Just. It's always hard to drag yourself out of bed when you're on nights, isn't it?' he replied, trying not to dwell on the thought of why Katie might feel uncomfortable around him because it would only create problems...

Did Katie feel uneasy because she was *aware* of him, too? the part of his mind that refused to co-operate demanded, and a second sprout shot down the wrong way. Nick turned beetroot-red as he spluttered inelegantly into his paper napkin and he saw Katie look at him in concern.

'Are you all right?'

'Fine, apart from trying to choke myself on the veg,' he gurgled, feeling like a total idiot. He managed to clear the obstruction and smiled wanly at the rest of the group, who were all staring at him now. 'I'll make sure I chew everything twenty times from now on like my mother taught me to do.'

'Don't you worry about it. We're all trained in the art of CPR, aren't we, girls?' The nurse from the children's ward, who'd told him her name was Mel, winked at him. 'If you need the kiss of life then I'm sure one of us would be *more* than happy to oblige!'

Nick summoned a smile as everyone laughed but he felt a little embarrassed about Katie overhearing the comment. He shot her a rueful glance when the conversation moved on to a different topic. 'Sorry about that. My fault for choking on the wretched sprout in the first place.'

'There's no need to worry on my account,' she replied airily, cutting a sliver of turkey and popping it into her mouth.

It was obvious that she didn't want to discuss the matter so Nick turned his attention back to his meal but his appetite seemed to have disappeared all of a sudden. Didn't Katie *care* if the other woman found him attractive? he wondered dejectedly then had to swallow his groan of dismay when he realised how stupid it was to think like that. He'd come to Dalverston to do a job and that was all he should be concerned about, not whether or not Katie liked him enough to feel jealous because another woman had paid him attention. He stood up abruptly, because he knew it was time he nipped these feelings in the bud.

'Thanks for letting me sit with you. No doubt I'll see you all around the hospital at some point in the future.'

'You can count on it,' Mel replied, grinning at him.

Nick just smiled because it seemed safer than actually saying anything. He made a hasty exit, stacking his tray in the rack before leaving the canteen. He paused in the corridor, wondering what he should do next. It was just gone two and the afternoon stretched before him. He needed to fill in the time somehow so he decided to unload his car then go to the maternity unit. He needed a pager in case anyone wanted to get in touch with him so he'd see if they had one to spare.

That should fill in a couple of hours and stop him thinking about things he had no right to think about. He mustn't make the mistake of thinking that he and Katie could be more than colleagues because it wouldn't work. He didn't *do* commitment because he didn't have the time. Work took up the best part of his life and what little free time he had after that wasn't enough to build a proper relationship.

That was why he'd only ever had affairs in the past and that would never be enough for Katie. OK, so maybe he *was* jumping the gun, especially after what she'd said about her last boyfriend, but Nick knew in his heart that Katie was every bit as aware of him as he was of her. Even though it didn't prove she wanted to get to know him better it was best to be safe. He had to be strong from now on, possibly for Katie's sake, and *definitely* for his own.

Katie finished her lunch but the turkey tasted like saw-dust all of a sudden. She wasn't sure what had happened but she sensed that Nick's abrupt departure had had something to do with her. It was worrying to wonder what she'd done to upset him so she was glad when the party broke up. Mel caught up with her as she was leaving the canteen, linking her arm through Katie's as they made their way along the corridor.

'Right, I want to know *everything* about your new registrar, so when did he start?'

'Yesterday,' Katie replied shortly because she really didn't feel like discussing Nick at that moment.

'Really? How come?' Mel demanded. 'I mean, who's ever heard of a registrar *starting* work on Christmas Eve?'

'It was Nick's decision. He wasn't actually due to start work until after Christmas but we had an emergency and he offered his services.'

'Wow! Handsome *and* dedicated.' Mel placed her hand on her chest. 'Oh, be still, my beating heart!'

'I don't suppose he felt that he had much choice,'

Katie pointed out. She loved Mel dearly but there was no denying that she felt uneasy, talking about Nick.

'Maybe not but he still stepped in to help. I can think of a lot of people who wouldn't have bothered, emergency or not.'

Mel sounded so grim all of a sudden that Katie stared at her in surprise. 'Anyone in particular you're referring to?'

'That creep Gary Hutchins.'

'Isn't he the new junior registrar who started on Paeds last month?'

'That's the one.' Mel shuddered. 'There ought to be a law against employing men like him. Not only is he a waste of space when it comes to work, but he's such a lech! D'you know he trapped me in the sluice room the other day and if Sister hadn't come along heaven knows what would have happened. I tell you, Katie, he really scared me.'

'Did you report him?' Katie asked, forgetting her concerns when she saw how worried Mel looked. She sighed when her friend shook her head. 'Why ever not?'

'Because Gary would only have twisted it round to make it look as though he was the innocent party. He did it before in his last job and the nurse he came onto there ended up on a disciplinary charge.' Mel glowered. 'I'm certainly not putting *my* career on the line for the likes of him, not when I'm hoping to get the junior sister's job that's coming up soon.'

'Something should be done about him, though,' Katie said anxiously. 'If he's tried it on with you then he'll try it on with someone else and it might not end so happily the next time.'

'With a bit of luck the next girl Gary corners will have a boyfriend who'll sort him out good and proper.'

Mel held up her hand when Katie started to protest. 'No. I know you mean well, Katie, but I'm not going to report him so you can save your breath. I shall just keep well out of his way in future and advise you to do the same.'

Katie sighed as Mel hurried away. She couldn't *make* her friend report the incident if she didn't want to but it seemed wrong that the registrar should get away with what he'd done. She decided to speak to Niall about it when she got the chance. Maybe Niall could have a word with Mark Dawson, the head of Paediatrics, and get him to deal with the problem.

She felt a little happier after that and went back to her room to fetch her coat. It was a cold, crisp day and a stroll by the river might help to walk off her lunch. She left the staff quarters, following the path that led through the fields behind the hospital. From there it was just a short walk to the river so she set off, striding briskly over the grass. There were quite a lot of people about when she got there, most of them probably walking off the effects of their Christmas dinners as well. Katie strolled along the riverbank, wishing that she'd remembered to bring some bread for the ducks who were paddling along beside her. She came to a bend in the path and paused for a moment, debating whether to continue. The daylight was starting to fade and she didn't want to walk back across the fields in the dark.

She decided to head back and had turned round when a whimpering noise coming from the bushes beside the path made her stop. Katie stood and listened, and heard the sound again. Crossing the path, she bent down and parted the bushes then gasped in dismay. There was a baby in a cardboard box, and obviously newborn, too. He'd been wrapped in a blanket and covered with layers of newspaper but he was blue with cold. Katie quickly stripped off her coat and wrapped the baby inside it so that only his nose and mouth were showing. Although the coat would help to warm him, he desperately needed to go in an incubator. It was impossible to tell how long he'd been there but even a short period of time in the cold could prove fatal for a baby as young as this.

She hurried up the path and across the fields, heading straight to the maternity unit when she reached the hospital. Visiting hour had just finished so she had to ring the bell and her heart lurched when Nick appeared to let her in. She hadn't expected to see him again that day but obviously he'd decided to spend some time in work again.

'I found a baby down by the river,' she explained as she hurried inside. 'I don't know how long he's been there but he's very cold.'

'Take him straight through,' Nick instructed, not wasting time by asking her any questions. 'I'll phone SCBU and tell them what's happened then check him over.'

'Fine.' Katie hurried to the examination room and laid the baby on the bed. They kept a heated crib on standby so she checked it was ready then put some towels and blankets to warm, and by that time Nick had arrived.

'Rosie is going to phone the police and tell them what's happened,' he told her, coming straight over to the bed and unwrapping her coat from around the infant. He quickly checked the child's limbs and listened to his heart, felt his skull and examined his eyes. 'He seems fine apart from the fact that he's so cold.'

'He'll soon warm up once we get him into that crib,' Katie murmured, swaddling the tiny body in a warm blanket then popping a bonnet onto his head to help contain his meagre store of body heat. She picked him up and cuddled him, wondering how anyone could have parted with something so precious as this tiny child.

'The mother must have been in a pretty bad way to have left him like that,' Nick observed softly, and she looked at him in surprise.

'I don't know how anyone could just abandon a baby like that,' she said shortly, because it was unsettling to wonder if he'd read her mind.

'I don't suppose the mother wanted to abandon him but she might have felt that she had no choice,' Nick said quietly as she carried the baby to the crib and settled him inside. He shrugged when she glanced at him in surprise. 'I'm not condoning her actions, Katie, but let's not be too hard on her until we find out something more about her circumstances. Some situations are a lot more complicated than they first appear to be.'

He looked round when Rosie popped her head round the door to tell them the police had arrived and wanted to speak to Katie. 'Can you tell them that she'll be there in a minute, please, Rosie?' he instructed, then turned to Katie again. 'I'll take this little fellow up to SCBU while you deal with the police. I expect they'll want to take a statement from you.'

Katie sighed as she went to the door. 'There's not much I can tell them. It was sheer good luck that I happened to be there and heard the poor little scrap crying.'

'Talk about being in the right place at the right time,' he observed lightly, wheeling the crib across the room. He smiled at her and Katie felt her heart swell when she saw the warmth in his hazel eyes. 'This little chap owes you his life, Katie, so I hope you feel proud of what you've done today.'

'Only as proud as you must feel for saving Karen's baby,' she pointed out, not wanting to get too carried away by the compliment. His smile faded abruptly and once again there was that bleakness in his eyes that she'd seen once before.

'I can't take any credit for that. It's a miracle that we didn't end up with a tragedy on our hands thanks to my selfishness.'

'Selfishness? That's a bit strong, Nick. You weren't even supposed to be here.'

'Maybe not, but I should have had more sense than to play stupid games.'

He didn't wait for her to reply as he pushed the crib out of the room. Katie followed him along the corridor, veering off to go to the office while he continued towards the lift. Quite frankly, she found his attitude very surprising for a number of reasons. She'd seen him operate yesterday and his skill certainly wasn't in doubt. She'd also seen how he'd behaved during the carol concert and he hadn't acted like a man who suffered from a lack of confidence yet he seemed intent on blaming himself when there was no need. Katie found herself wondering why he was so hard on himself for so little apparent reason. Had something dreadful happened in Nick's past, something he blamed himself for?

She sighed when it struck her how silly it was to let her imagination run away with her. Fantasising about Nick Lawson's past life was the last thing she should be doing if she hoped to keep her feet firmly on the ground!

CHAPTER FOUR

BY THE time the police had taken a statement from Katie and asked her to accompany them back to the river to show them where she'd found the baby, it was time for her to go on duty. Rosie was obviously keen to get away so they did the handover as quickly as possible then Katie went to check on the mums who'd delivered that day. There were four in all which was a record for the unit. Last year they'd not had a single baby born on Christmas Day so it was exciting for the staff as well as for the parents.

Katie went to M1 first, the largest of the four maternity wards. There were six beds in the ward and all were occupied. December was always a busy month and even though they tried to discharge as many new mums as possible in time for Christmas, some needed that little extra care and had to remain in hospital over the holiday.

Katie had a word with each of the women in turn then went to see their newest addition. Debbie Mills had had a little girl so Katie admired her and congratulated the parents. Debbie looked tired but ecstatic as she stared at her tiny daughter lying in the crib beside her.

'I still can't believe she's real! I know that must sound really daft after I've just given birth to her, but I keep thinking I'll wake up and find it's all been a dream.'

'Wait until she's crying for her night-time feeds,' Katie warned her, smiling. 'You'll soon come back down to earth with a bump then!'

Debbie laughed. 'That's what that lovely new doctor said when he came to visit me before. What was his name now…? Oh, yes, Dr Lawson. Mind you, he did say that it would be worth all the sleepless nights, didn't he, Martin?' she added, turning to her husband.

'I think it was more a case of him wanting to make sure we didn't try and send her back,' the young man said with a grin.

Katie laughed but she was surprised that Nick had been to check on Debbie. Bearing in mind that he wasn't rostered for work yet, there'd been no need for him to do so. However, it was the same story with all the new mums she visited. Every one mentioned that Nick had been to see her and they all remarked how lovely he was, too.

As she went to the office to catch up with some of the paperwork that needed doing, Katie couldn't help wondering if there was something odd about such extreme dedication. Granted, every single person who worked in the department gave one hundred per cent effort, but few would have volunteered to work on their days off unless it was in an emergency. Nick seemed to be carrying his commitment just a bit too far and it bothered her, although she wasn't sure why exactly. Maybe it was that idea she'd had earlier—that he blamed himself for something that had happened and was trying to atone for it.

If that was true then his life must be very difficult and it hurt in a way she would never have expected, to imagine Nick suffering that way. Crazy though it sounded after such a short acquaintance, she hated to think that he was unhappy.

*   *   *

The evening flew past and midnight came and went. There were no new admissions so Katie let Abbey and Ruth take their meal breaks together. She'd just settled down to the January staffing rosters when the bell went and she sighed because it was typical that it should happen when the other midwives had gone to the canteen.

Katie hurried to the front door and opened it. There was a car parked under the awning and she ran outside when she heard a woman screaming. A young man was crouched down beside the rear door of the vehicle so Katie went straight to him.

'What's happened?' she demanded, moving him aside so she could see into the car. There was a young woman lying hunched up on the back seat and she was obviously very distressed.

'I don't know! Lara's been having pains on and off all day long but she wanted to see her parents so we decided to stick to our plans and drive over here to visit them.' The young man ran a trembling hand over his face. 'The pains started getting worse after supper so we thought we'd better go home. Her mum wanted to phone for an ambulance but Lara wouldn't hear of it. She insisted that she wanted to have the baby at home as we'd arranged. Then just as we were about to join the motorway, she started screaming that she was in terrible pain so I brought her straight here.'

'You did exactly the right thing,' Katie assured him. 'Now, see if you can help Lara out of the car while I fetch a wheelchair for her.'

She ran back inside and collected one of the chairs then went back to the car. The young woman was on her feet now but she was obviously in tremendous pain. Katie helped her into the chair and took her straight to a delivery room. Getting her onto the bed was a struggle but she managed it with the help of the girl's partner. She glanced at him as she took a stethoscope off the trolley.

'When's her due date, do you know?'

'First of January,' he replied promptly, his face turning rather green when the young woman began screaming again.

Katie decided that she didn't have the time to deal with him if he fainted and nodded to the door. 'Can you wait outside while I examine her? It won't take long.'

'Yes. Right. Sure,' he gabbled, hastily backing out of the room.

Katie turned her attention to the young woman as soon as he'd left. 'I'm just going to check your baby's heartbeat, Lara. There's nothing to worry about.'

'It...*hurts!*' the girl wailed.

'I know and I'll give you something for the pain in a moment, love,' Katie assured her, helping the girl to lie down. It took her a moment to find the baby's heartbeat and she grimaced. Draping the stethoscope around her neck, she carefully felt the mother's tummy and realised her suspicions were correct. The baby was lying transversely across the uterus and the intense pain Lara had been experiencing stemmed from the fact that the infant's arm and shoulder were becoming jammed in her pelvis. The child simply couldn't be born in that position and each fresh contraction merely exacerbated the problem. It was a highly dangerous situation for both mother and child so Katie didn't hesitate as she went to the phone and asked the switchboard to page Nick then contacted Theatre and put them on standby.

She helped Lara undress and put on a gown, quietening her fears as best she could. It would be up to Nick to explain that she would need a Caesarean section so Katie was glad when he arrived a few minutes later. She went to meet him at the door so she could explain the problem without Lara overhearing what they said.

'Thanks for coming so quickly. The patient's name is Lara Henderson and she's due on the first of January. That's all I know about her because she isn't one of our patients. I've had a quick look at her and the baby's transverse from what I can tell.'

'It will need to be a section, then,' Nick confirmed, glancing across the room. 'Have you told her yet?'

'No, I thought I'd leave it to you to do that. She might have some questions for you.'

'Right, I'll go and break the news to her. Can you warn Theatre for me?'

'I've already done it,' Katie assured him, and he grinned.

'Mind reader!'

Katie didn't say anything. She certainly didn't want to go into the ins and outs of whether or not she could read his mind because it would be far too unsettling. She phoned the canteen and asked to speak to Ruth, apologising for interrupting her break before explaining the situation to her. Once she was sure the other midwife was on her way back she was free to concentrate on what needed doing.

Nick was still talking to Lara and Katie frowned when she realised that all wasn't well. She listened in mounting dismay as the young woman refused to give her consent for the section to take place. Even though Lara was in a great deal of pain, she was adamant about not having it.

'No! I don't want a section. I've been to all the

classes and I know what to do. I want to have my baby by myself!'

'Nobody can force you to undergo a procedure you don't want, Miss Henderson,' Nick said quietly, but Katie shivered when she heard the steely edge in his voice. It was obvious that Nick took a dim view of the young woman's refusal to co-operate and she really couldn't blame him.

'At the end of the day, the decision has to lie with you. All I can do is warn you of the consequences for both you and your child.'

'But I wanted a natural birth, not someone cutting me open,' Lara insisted. 'Don't you understand? I had it all planned and this wasn't how it was supposed to happen!'

'I do understand. And I appreciate how hard it must be to accept that you can't have the sort of birth you'd hoped for. However, your child's welfare is the most important issue here, surely?' Nick said firmly. 'Your baby is lying horizontally across your uterus and there is no way that he can be born like that. His arm and shoulder simply aren't able to pass through your pelvis from that position. You have to trust me when I say that a section is the only way to resolve this problem.'

'How do I know you're not just saying that? You hear all those stories about women being forced to have operations they don't need,' Lara wailed, tears streaming down her face.

'And I am just as opposed to that kind of thinking as you are,' Nick said calmly, although Katie could sense his frustration. 'Childbirth should be a wonderful experience for a woman, but sometimes she needs help and this is one such occasion, I'm afraid.'

'I'm not sure…' Lara grimaced as another wave of

pain racked her body. She waited until it had subsided before she continued in a quavering voice. 'You swear there's no way that I can have this baby by myself?'

'Yes, I swear. It's far too late to turn it and your only option now is a Caesarean section. Everything is ready so all we need is your permission then we can go ahead.'

'I want to speak to John first,' she insisted stubbornly. 'My boyfriend.'

'Fine. I'll be outside when you've made up your mind.'

Nick turned on his heel and strode out of the room and a few seconds later the young man appeared. Katie moved aside so the couple could discuss what they were going to do in private, but she too was seething with impatience. When Ruth tapped on the door, she asked her to stay with the couple while she went to find Nick and see if there was anything else they could do to make the parents see sense. He was pacing the corridor and the expression on his face proved just how concerned he was.

'I can't believe how stubborn people can be!' he exploded when Katie went over to him.

'I know. It's incredible, isn't it?' She sighed as she glanced towards the delivery room. 'I'm just hoping the boyfriend can persuade her it's their only option.'

'Me, too.' Nick ran his hand through his hair. 'I'm sorry. I know I should be a bit more sympathetic, but it's hard when I think of all the women who've died in childbirth because they didn't have access to any proper medical facilities. That girl is playing roulette with her baby's life and all because someone has fed her a load of guff about natural childbirth being the only acceptable way of giving birth.'

'I'm sure Lara will come round to the idea,' Katie said soothingly, mentally crossing her fingers. 'A lot of mums get it into their heads that they're going to do this or that and find it difficult to adjust their ideas when the time comes. Fortunately, most forget their disappointment once they have their babies in their arms.'

'Your middle name doesn't happen to be Pollyanna, does it?' He grinned at her, his hazel eyes so full of warmth that an answering warmth flowed through her body.

'How did you guess?' she said lightly because she was terrified he'd notice her response. 'I'm one of the world's optimists, although I don't know whether that's a good thing or a bad. Looking on the bright side all the time has a tendency to drive everyone around you crazy.'

'Well, you certainly don't drive me crazy, Katie. In fact, I'd go so far as to say that I wish some of your optimism would rub off on me. I could certainly do with looking on the bright side for a change.'

Nick couldn't believe he'd said that. Normally, he steered clear of discussing his own feelings but there was something about Katie that broke down the barriers he'd erected between himself and the world. He seemed to respond to her on a different level than with anyone else and it was scary to face that fact. It was a relief when the delivery room door opened and Lara's boyfriend appeared.

Nick went to meet him, deliberately focusing all his attention on the current situation rather than the way he'd been behaving recently. It was certainly grim enough to warrant it yet he couldn't pretend he wasn't aware of Katie when she came to join them. It took a vast amount of effort to blot out the signals whizzing to his brain, messages about how warm her skin felt when their arms brushed, how delicious the scent of her shampoo smelt. It was as though every cell in his body was suddenly conscious of every cell in hers and it was hard to behave as though everything was normal when it most certainly wasn't, only he didn't have a choice.

'Lara told me what you said, Doctor, about the baby being all jammed inside her and that the only way for it to be born is for her to have a Caesarean section,' John said in a shocked voice.

'That's right. Believe me, I would never advocate a section unless there was a valid reason for it and, in this instance, there is,' Nick said firmly because he couldn't afford to start wavering about work or anything else. 'Bluntly, both the baby and Lara could die unless we do something soon.'

John blanched. 'In that case I don't think we have much choice, do we? She'll have to have the operation.'

'Yes.' Nick clapped him on the shoulder. 'Everything is ready so now we just need Lara's signature on the relevant form and we can get this over with.'

'Give it to me and I'll make sure she signs it for you,' John offered immediately.

Nick glanced at Katie, trying desperately to ignore the spasm that passed through him when he saw the relief in her soft grey eyes. 'Can you get the paperwork sorted out then scrub up? I'd like you to assist me again if you wouldn't mind.'

'Of course.'

Nick left her to deal with it but his heart was heavy as he made his way to Theatre. The relief he'd seen on Katie's face had mirrored his own feelings so perfectly that it felt as though another bond had been forged between them and he knew how dangerous it was to think like that. His contract at Dalverston was for three months, with an option to stay a further three months if he and the management were happy with the arrangement.

He'd been planning on staying the full six months because Dalverston's obstetric department was renowned for its high standards and the experience he gained there would be invaluable to him. Now, however, Nick realised that he would have to alter his plans. There was no point making his life even more difficult when every minute he spent with Katie only seemed to increase his awareness of her so he would leave at the end of the initial three months and just hope that he wouldn't do anything foolish between now and then.

Larry, the anaesthetist he'd worked with the previous day, was already in Theatre when Nick arrived, and he grinned when he saw Nick coming through the door. 'Not you again! How come you managed to draw the short straw and ended up working all over Christmas?'

'Just lucky, I guess,' Nick replied lightly, trying to clear his mind as he started to scrub up. He knew what he had to do and now he must stick to it, no matter how difficult it might prove to be.

'You and me both. Makes you wonder if we've done something really wicked in a former life, doesn't it?' Larry observed cheerfully.

Their patient arrived just then so there was no time for any more chit-chat. Nick went straight into Theatre while Larry set about anaesthetising Lara in readiness for the operation. She was having a general anaesthetic and it didn't take long to give her the premed before she was wheeled into Theatre and transferred to the operating table.

Katie followed her in and Nick nodded to her then

determinedly turned his attention to the task at hand. This was what he was here for and everything else was inconsequential. As he made the first incision, Nick experienced a rush of relief because now he knew exactly what he was doing.

He was saving a life—possibly two—and that was all he'd wanted to do since Mike had died. Maybe Katie *did* arouse a wealth of emotions inside him but he would deal with them the only way he knew—by blocking them out. It wasn't worth all the heartache to let himself hope for anything more than he had, certainly wasn't right to wish that Katie could become a permanent part of his life. He'd known her only a couple of days and it was far too early to start thinking along those lines.

The night finally came to an end and Katie had to admit that she was relieved when it was time to go off duty. Although it hadn't been a particularly busy night, it had been a stressful one. Fortunately, the Caesarean had been textbook-perfect and Lara was now sleeping peacefully in a side room while her baby—a healthy little boy—was in the nursery, none the worse for his ordeal. Katie popped in to see him before she left, smiling when she heard him crying lustily in his cot. There certainly didn't seem to be much wrong with his lungs, although it could have been a very different story if Nick hadn't persuaded the parents to see sense.

She sighed as she let herself out of the nursery and walked to the lift. In the space of thirty-six hours Nick had saved the lives of two mothers and their babies. There was no doubt that he was a highly skilled doctor but she found it hard to understand him as a person. He seemed such a contradiction—joking one minute, serious the next—that it was difficult to slot him into any sort of category. Maybe she should just accept him as he was but she'd feel easier if she understood him better.

Katie went to her room and got ready for bed, but once again she found it difficult to settle. She finally fell into a light doze around eight o'clock but was awake again by eleven and knew there was no hope of going back to sleep after that. She got dressed then decided to make herself some breakfast for a treat. There was a kitchen on each floor and, although the facilities were basic, she could at least rustle up some bacon and eggs for herself.

She had just started frying the bacon when footsteps in the corridor made her turn round and her heart jolted when she saw Nick standing in the doorway. He was dressed in frayed jeans and a bobbly old sweater and there were dark circles under his eyes, but none of that mattered a jot. He was so drop-dead gorgeous that her insides suddenly started melting with lust and it was scary to feel this way after what had happened between her and David.

She'd always known what she wanted from life—marriage, a family and the kind of relationship that lasted a lifetime. David hadn't wanted any of those things but she'd allowed the physical attraction she'd felt for him to blind her to that fact so it was doubly alarming to have to deal with these feelings for Nick. It took every scrap of effort she could summon not to let him see how worried she felt when he grinned at her.

'There ought to be a law against people frying bacon at this time of the day.' He groaned. 'It's nothing short of torture to be woken up by that delicious smell!'

'Sorry.' Katie cleared her throat, hoping he couldn't tell how edgy she felt. 'I thought I'd make myself some breakfast for a treat. Normally, I make do with a piece of toast when I'm on night duty.'

'Me, too. I have all these good intentions about cooking for myself but usually I'm too tired to bother. Thank heaven for staff canteens is all I can say.'

'That must be a first.' She laughed, feeling some of her tension ease when it soon became obvious that he hadn't noticed anything odd about her behaviour. 'I've never heard anyone extol the delights of canteen food before.'

'No? Then they must never have had to eat some of the meals I've been served over the years.' He grinned at her. 'If it walks, crawls, flies or swims then I've probably eaten it.'

'Oh, yuck! I don't think I want to hear any more. Some things are definitely best kept to yourself.'

'Are you sure?' He chuckled, his hazel eyes alight with laughter, and, despite her good intentions, Katie felt her heart start to bounce around inside her chest like a ping-pong ball. 'I could give you my recipe for iguana stew, if you like. It's quite tasty, actually, so long as you make sure that you remove all the claws before you dish it up.'

'Stop it! I'm not listening to you!' She put her hands over her ears but he wasn't deterred.

'But I was going to tell you how to make cockroach pudding next,' he said, trying—and failing—to look suitably hurt. 'Are you sure you don't want the recipe?'

'Quite sure,' she retorted, glaring at him.

'It's up to you, of course.' He sighed reproachfully. 'I just never imagined you'd have such a closed mind, Katie.'

'It's not my mind I'm concerned about but my poor stomach,' she returned tartly, flipping over the bacon before it started to burn. 'I hate to disillusion you but I like my food to come all nicely packaged from the supermarket. That way I know exactly what I'm eating.'

'You don't know what you're missing.'

'Oh, yes, I do! Iguana stew and roach pudding are two treats I'll happily pass on.'

She lowered the heat under the pan then looked at him curiously. Maybe this wasn't the best time to start delving into Nick's past but she couldn't resist finding out more about him. 'How come you've eaten all those things, anyway? Surely it wasn't out of choice?'

'No, it wasn't, but it's amazing what you'll eat when you're really hungry,' he said dryly, sitting down at the table. 'I do a lot of work for that aid agency I told you about so I spend quite a bit of time abroad each year. Most of the places we work have very few resources so we share whatever supplies we have with the local people. Once all our canned and dried goods run out we have to eat whatever's available until the next lot arrives. Sometimes it takes just a few days to get a shipment through but at other times it can take weeks, hence the rather unusual menus.'

He tipped back his chair and smiled at her, and Katie felt her heart perform another of those crazy bouncing acts, tumbling about inside her chest so that she felt quite giddy.

'You mentioned something about India,' she said, desperately trying to appear as though nothing was happening—no mean feat in the circumstances. 'Was that where you were before you accepted this post?'

'Uh-huh. I think I told you that I was helping to set up a new maternity unit there?' He carried on when she nodded. 'The area where we were working is very remote so the women there have had to rely on the village midwives in the past. Birth control is virtually unheard of so most women have umpteen pregnancies during their lifetimes and, sadly, a large percentage of them end as stillbirths.'

'How awful! It's easy to forget that there are still many parts of the world where there's no proper antenatal care available, isn't it? We're lucky in the UK because every single woman here has access to a range of facilities to help her during her pregnancy.'

'That's right. It's even more heartbreaking when you think that in many of the poorer countries it's the small things that make such a huge difference—staff who understand about the dangers of infection, for instance. Just drumming it into people that they must wash their hands and keep everything clean can work wonders.'

'So that was part of your remit, was it? Setting up a code of good nursing practice?' she asked in surprise, because she wouldn't have expected a doctor as highly skilled as Nick to involve himself in anything so basic.

'Amongst other things, yes. Good nursing practice is absolutely vital. You can have the best facilities in the world but they're not worth a red cent if people don't appreciate the dangers of not following the basic rules of hygiene. We were very selective about who we chose to work in the new unit once it was completed but I think we managed to get a good team together in the end. Now all we can hope is that it will make a difference to the local people's lives.'

'Do you monitor the situation or just leave it to the local staff once you've set everything up?' she asked, lifting the bacon out of the pan and putting it on some kitchen paper to drain while she fried the eggs. She broke two into the pan in case Nick decided to join her for breakfast then had to take a deep breath because the thought of them sharing breakfast was a little too intimate for some reason.

'We usually appoint a local physician to oversee the project,' he explained. 'Shiloh also sends someone out to do spot checks every so often.'

'Shiloh?' She looked at him in surprise. 'You don't mean Shiloh Smith, do you?'

'Yes. Why? Do you know him?'

'Oh, yes! He's married to one of my best friends—Rachel Hart,' she exclaimed. 'She used to be the sister on the children's ward until she left to have a baby.'

'Of course! I'd forgotten that Rachel used to work at Dalverston General.' He grinned at her. 'Small world, isn't it?'

'It is indeed,' Katie agreed, smiling back. There was a moment when their eyes met and her breath caught because it felt as though she and Nick were suddenly communicating on a whole new level. It was as though they had a direct line into each other's thoughts and it was a shock to experience this kind of closeness with him. She took a half-step towards him then stopped when he suddenly stood up.

'Well, pleasant though it's been, chatting to you, this isn't getting my car cleaned. It's in a real state after the drive up from London so I thought I'd better make the effort and wash it.' He grimaced. 'I don't suppose you know where I can find a bucket, do you? I've hunted through all the cupboards upstairs but I couldn't find one anywhere.'

'I...um... Yes, of course.'

Katie turned away and went to the broom cupboard but her hands were shaking as she opened the door. Had

Nick felt that moment of closeness, too, and was that why he'd broken the spell?

She sensed it was so and she couldn't help feeling hurt by his deliberate rejection. She quickly crouched down and scrabbled through the contents of the cupboard because she didn't want him to see that she was upset. If Nick didn't want to foster a closer relationship with her that was his choice.

'Will this do?' she said, dragging out an old bucket and showing it to him.

'Yes, that's great. Thanks.' He took it from her and went to the sink. Turning on the tap, he filled the bucket with hot water and added a dollop of dish detergent then glanced round. 'Sorry to be a pest, but I don't suppose you've got a sponge in there as well, have you?'

'I'll have a look.' Katie delved into the cupboard again and spotted a rather ragged sponge wedged into a back corner. She picked it up then let out a shriek when a huge black spider ran over the back of her hand.

'What's the matter? Katie, what have you done?' Nick hauled her to her feet so fast that she had to clutch hold of his arms to stop herself falling over.

'I'm all right. It was just a spider. It ran across my hand when I picked up the sponge.' She shuddered convulsively and he laughed softly.

'Don't tell me you're scared of spiders? I don't believe it. No elf worth her salt is afraid of *spiders*!'

'Well, this particular elf is!' she shot back, glaring up at him—only somehow her scowl ended up getting sidetracked along the way.

Katie felt a shiver of excitement dance its way down her spine when she saw the light in Nick's eyes. He was staring at her as though she was the most wonderful sight he'd seen in a very long time, and she couldn't begin to explain how that made her feel. When his head started to dip she could feel her heart pounding because she just knew he was going to kiss her...

CHAPTER FIVE

'OH, YUM! Is that bacon I can smell frying?'

Katie nearly jumped out of her skin when Mel came bounding into the kitchen. She dredged up a smile as Nick quickly released her but she was trembling when she turned to her friend. 'It is. I might have known your taste buds would lead you here. D'you want some?'

'Please—so long as I'm not interrupting anything?'

Katie flushed when she saw the speculation on Mel's face. 'Of course you aren't. Nick was just about to go outside and wash his car. Weren't you, Nick?'

'That's right.'

He lifted the bucket out of the sink and grinned at them. Katie felt a knot of pain grip her heart because he didn't seem upset about the sudden interruption. Had she misread the situation, perhaps?

'It's my least favourite job, too, but as Katie has very kindly found me a bucket, I've no excuse now not to get it done.' He dropped the sponge into the soapy water then saluted them smartly. 'Farewell, sweet ladies. 'Tis a far, far better thing I do now, etcetera, etcetera.'

'Idiot!' Mel retorted, smiling at him.

Katie turned away because she couldn't bear to see how Nick would respond to her friend's overtures. She'd thought he'd wanted to kiss her just now because she was special, but maybe she'd assumed too much. After all, he had told her about the long periods he spent abroad and it was doubtful if he had much female company while he was away. He probably would have be-

71

haved the same way with *any* woman just now and the thought was so painful that it was hard to hide her dismay when Mel immediately launched into a discussion about Nick's love life as soon as he'd left.

'You've spoken to him more than anyone else has, Katie, so what's he told you?' Mel demanded, tucking into the bacon and egg Katie had placed in front of her with relish. 'Has he mentioned a girlfriend to you?'

'No, but most of our conversations have been about work,' Katie replied shortly, sitting down.

'Pity.' Mel sighed. 'It would be so much easier if we knew something about him, wouldn't it?'

'I know that he's been working overseas,' Katie volunteered because she felt mean about withholding the information. After all, it wasn't Mel's fault if Nick was a bit of a flirt, was it? Her stomach lurched at the thought and she hurried on.

'He was in India for quite a while from what I can gather. In fact, that was where he was before he came to Dalverston. He spent some months working over there, setting up a new maternity unit.'

'Really?' Mel's expression brightened. 'Doesn't sound as though he has a "significant other", does it? I mean, he'd hardly have spent all that time abroad if he was in a proper relationship. And the fact that he's moved all the way to Dalverston is another indication that he's not attached. He'd have stayed in London if there was someone special in his life.'

'You could be right.' Katie got up and plugged in the kettle, hoping Mel would let the subject drop. She'd never even considered the possibility that Nick might be involved with anyone else and it shocked her that she'd given no thought to something so important.

'I hope I am, but there's an easy way to find out, of

course,' Mel declared, grinning like a cat who'd just been offered a dish of cream. 'I think this calls for action, don't you?'

'What do you mean?' Katie demanded, turning to look at her friend.

Mel laughed. 'What do you think I mean? Oh, come on, Katie, you've got to admit that Nick Lawson is the first eligible male we've had working in this place for *ages*! OK, I know that you don't go in for flings because you're still hoping for the love, marriage and happily-ever-after scenario, but I'm not like you. I want to have a bit of fun while I'm still young enough to enjoy myself and Nick strikes me as the ideal candidate to have it with. I just need to give him a nudge in the right direction and I know the perfect way to do it, too. I'm going to invite him to the New Year's Eve ball!'

'He might already have made plans for New Year,' Katie said, trying to hide her dismay. She certainly didn't have the right to vet who Mel dated, but the thought of her going to the ball with Nick was almost more than she could bear.

'I doubt it,' Mel scoffed. 'I mean, he's hardly going to drive all the way back to London for one night, is he? No, I'm going to ask him if he'd like to go to the ball and see what he says.' She pushed back her chair and stood up. 'Wish me luck?'

'Of course.'

Katie managed to smile but she was glad when Mel left because she doubted if she could have kept up the pretence for much longer. She cleared everything away then went to fetch her coat. A lot of the shops were starting their after-Christmas sales that day so she'd go into town and see if she could find herself any bargains.

At least it would give her something to do until it was time to report for duty.

She took a short cut through the car park and had almost reached the gates when she spotted Mel and Nick standing beside his car. They were both laughing and Katie quickly turned away before they noticed her. It was obvious they were getting along famously so she could only assume that Mel's plan had worked. Maybe she should be happy for her friend but, as she made her way to the bus stop, Katie realised that she'd have given anything to be the one going to the ball with Nick on New Year's Eve.

'It's really kind of you to invite me but I'm not sure yet if I'll be working over New Year. Can I let you know?'

Nick dredged up a smile when Mel told him cheerfully that she'd check back with him later and hurried away. At least she didn't seem upset by his answer and that was something to be thankful for. He sighed as he took the soapy sponge out of the bucket because at any other time he would have jumped at the chance of spending the evening with an attractive woman like Mel. Although he wasn't looking for commitment, he was a normal, healthy male and enjoyed female company as much as the next guy did. However, the thought of spending the evening with Mel when he *really* wanted to spend it with Katie was more than he could handle.

He cursed roundly as he set to work on his car because he certainly didn't want to feel like this. Car washing was a job he hated normally, but it was a relief to have something to vent his frustrations on that day. He finished the task in record time and took the bucket back inside, checking that there was nobody about before he went into the kitchen.

He stowed the bucket away in the cupboard, sighing as he recalled how close he'd come to breaking his self-imposed rules. If they hadn't been interrupted he would have kissed Katie and that would have been a terrible mistake. Although there was no doubt in his mind that Katie got to him in a way that no other woman had done, he couldn't use that as an excuse. Katie deserved more than a few weeks of passion, which was all he could offer her!

Thoroughly disgusted with himself, Nick went back to his room and changed. Although nobody was expecting him to work that day, it would help to take his mind off Katie if he had something to do. He just had to hang onto the thought that if he got through the next three months then he would be back on track, but it wasn't much comfort. He wasn't looking forward to leaving Dalverston when it meant that he would be leaving Katie, but what else could he do?

It had been his brother's dream to make a difference to people's lives and now that Mike was dead, he had to see it through. Maybe other people would think he was crazy but it was the only way he could cope with his guilt. Even though he couldn't change what had happened, he could at least try to make amends. There simply wasn't room in his life for Katie even though he wished there was.

The shops were packed with bargain hunters so Katie only stayed for an hour then went back to the hospital. She didn't feel like sitting in her room so she got changed into her uniform. Although there were a couple of hours left before she went on duty, Jean would probably appreciate an early finish.

It was teatime when she arrived at the maternity unit so she took over the task of pouring the tea. Everyone wanted to know why she'd come into work so early but she shrugged off the questions by explaining that she'd had nothing better to do. As soon as the patients had been served their meals, she went to the office and relieved Jean.

The handover was straightforward because there was nobody in the delivery rooms. They'd had just one new admission that day, in fact, a young woman called Amanda Green, who was four months pregnant and threatening to miscarry. She was one of their patients so Katie decided to check on her before she did anything else. Jean had put her in a side room so Katie tapped on the door and went in, only to come to a halt when she saw Nick standing by the bed. She'd had no idea that he would be there so it was a moment before she could gather her composure again.

'Hello, Amanda. How are you feeling?' she asked quietly, nodding to Nick as she went over to the bed.

'Scared.' Tears welled from the young woman's eyes. 'I've always been so healthy that it never crossed my mind that something like this could happen. I keep trying to work out what I've done wrong.'

'You haven't done anything wrong,' Nick corrected gently. 'So you must stop blaming yourself.'

He turned to Katie and his tone was strictly businesslike this time. 'We've done a scan and the baby is fine, which is the good news. Amanda has had some spotting and slight cramping but there's no sign that the amniotic sac has ruptured. I've examined her and it looks like an incompetent cervix is the cause of the problem. Her cervix is a couple of centimetres dilated.'

'Will you be able to put a stitch in it?' Katie asked evenly, following his lead.

'Yes, that's what I'm planning on doing. I was just about to explain the procedure to Amanda when you arrived.'

He turned back to the bed and Katie swallowed her sigh because it was obvious that Nick was keen to forget what had happened earlier. Even though she knew it was probably for the best, she couldn't help feeling disappointed. She made herself concentrate as he explained the procedure to Amanda because it was easier to think about that than her own feelings.

'Your cervix needs strengthening so I'm going to put a stitch in it to stop it opening any further,' he explained. 'It will be done under local anaesthetic using a spinal block, or epidural as it's more commonly known, so you shouldn't find it too uncomfortable.'

'I'm sorry, Doctor, but I'm not sure that I understand what you mean,' Amanda said hesitantly. 'The cervix is part of my womb, isn't it?'

'That's right.' Nick sat down on the edge of the bed and took a pen out of his pocket. Picking up the file from the bedside table, he drew a diagram on the back. 'This is the cervix here. It's a small cylindrical organ comprising the lower part and neck of the womb. It's made of fibrous tissue and muscle which forms a sphincter, which is just a fancy name for a circular muscle. Are you with me so far?'

'Yes.' Amanda managed a ghost of a smile. 'I really should have genned up on all this before.'

'Don't you worry about it,' Nick told her with a grin. 'That's my job so you can leave the anatomy to me.'

Katie sighed when Amanda laughed. Nick had a knack of putting people at their ease yet he wasn't anywhere near as easy on himself. Once again she was struck by the contradiction and it was alarming to realise that she was more curious than ever about him. She knew that she had to stop thinking about him all the time for her own peace of mind, but it was proving an almost impossible task.

'The cervix lengthens during pregnancy and acts as a barrier to keep the baby inside the womb. However, sometimes a weakness can develop and the cervix starts to open, which is what has happened to you. I'll put a suture—or stitch—round here and that should solve the problem.'

He showed Amanda the diagram and she studied it for a moment then frowned. 'But how will the baby be born if my cervix is stitched together?'

'I can remove the suture before your due date so you can deliver the baby vaginally. Or you could choose to have a section, if you prefer,' he told her.

'Which is best? For the baby, I mean?' she asked worriedly, and Nick smiled.

'You're not jumping onto the too-posh-to-push bandwagon then?'

Amanda laughed. 'Not unless I really have to! My sister had a section and it took her ages to recover from it afterwards. She was so sore that she could hardly bear to pick up her baby.'

'That can be the downside, although most mums are back on their feet in a week or so. Anyhow, you don't have to decide right this very minute. You can tell me what you want to do later on.'

'So you really think it will work?' Amanda asked hopefully.

'I can't guarantee it, of course, but there's a very good chance that you'll be able to carry the baby to term if I put this stitch in,' Nick assured her. 'I'll do it first thing tomorrow morning, which will give us time to see what's happening. If your cervix doesn't dilate any more we'll go ahead.'

'And if it does open up any further you won't be able to do anything?' Amanda asked in a small voice.

'If the cervix is more than four centimetres dilated then the chances of a viable pregnancy are greatly decreased, I'm afraid.' He patted her hand before he stood up. 'We're not at that stage yet so let's just keep our fingers crossed, shall we? Now, I want you to stay in bed and rest.'

He turned to Katie. 'Amanda's husband should be here very shortly so if you could send him to the office I can explain everything to him as well.'

'Of course,' Katie agreed politely. She made sure that Amanda was comfortable then left her to rest. Anita Walsh, the community midwife, was just booking in a patient when she reached Reception so Katie stopped and had a word with them. The mum was just booked in for the delivery and would be going home straight afterwards so Katie wished her well and carried on. There was a pile of reports that needed doing, plus the end-of-year figures needed collating, and this would be the ideal time to start on them. Yet she hesitated when she reached the office. Nick was in there and suddenly the thought of having to sit in the same room as him when her emotions were in such turmoil was more than she could face.

She swung round and headed back the way she'd come. She would leave the paperwork until a later date…

'Katie, hang on a second!'

Katie stopped and turned round when Nick came hurrying out of the office. 'Is something wrong?'

'A and E have just phoned. They've got a girl down there who's just been brought in by her parents. She's sixteen and suffering from heavy vaginal bleeding. She's refused to tell A and E anything but they're pretty sure that she's had a baby recently.'

'You think she might be the mother of that baby I found?' Katie exclaimed.

'I'd lay odds on it. It's too much of a coincidence, isn't it? Anyway, I'm going straight down to A and E to see her so could you get one of the side rooms ready, please? And can you keep it quiet, too?' His tone was grim. 'It appears the press have been hanging around and the last thing we need is them getting to hear about this. The poor kid has enough on her plate from the sound of it.'

'Of course,' Katie agreed in dismay. 'You were right, Nick. If it does turn out that she's the baby's mother I was wrong to prejudge her. The poor kid must have been scared stiff and I feel really terrible about what I said now.'

'Don't go blaming yourself,' he said quietly. 'You weren't to know, were you?'

'No, but I could have been a bit kinder,' she admitted guiltily.

'Katie, if more people were like you the world would be a much better place, believe me.'

He touched her lightly on the cheek then strode away. Katie bit her lip as she watched him hurrying to the stairs. He gave out such mixed signals that it was no wonder she felt confused. One minute he was pushing her away and the next... Well, the next he was behaving as though he really *felt* something for her. Was it just that he was an inveterate flirt and couldn't help coming on to a woman—the gentle touch, the intimate smile, the lingering eye contact? Or was there more to it than that? Did Nick really feel something for *her*, perhaps?

She spun round in a sudden fit of impatience because there was no time to stand there worrying about how Nick might or might not feel. If he had any real feelings for her he'd tell her so…

Wouldn't he?

A sudden chill ran through her because there was no guarantee that Nick would ever admit to his feelings.

'I'd like to get her straight to Theatre so can you arrange for a porter to take her upstairs, please? It looks as though part of the placenta has been retained and I'll need to get it sorted out as quickly as possible.'

Nick sighed when the young A and E nurse apologetically explained that there were no porters available at the moment. Even though it was Boxing Day, the accident and emergency unit was a hive of activity and the staff were struggling to cope.

'Don't worry about it,' he told her. 'I'll take her up myself as soon as I've had a word with her parents. If you could just let Theatre know that I'll be there in a few minutes that would be a real help.'

He peeled off his gloves and tossed them into the waste sack as the nurse hurried away. Jodie Carmichael was a very sick girl and he found it difficult to contain his anger as he went back to the bed. She was still refusing to admit that she'd had a baby and he found it absolutely deplorable that she was so afraid to tell the truth. He intended to find out why she was so terrified but first he needed to explain to Jodie what was going to happen.

'Hi, Jodie, how are you feeling now, sweetheart? Is the pain any better?'

'A bit,' she muttered, staring at him with terrified blue eyes.

'Good. The drugs I've given you will help a lot but I still need to get rid of all the stuff that's making you so ill. That means I'm going to take you to Theatre for an operation.'

'Will it hurt?' she asked, her lower lip wobbling ominously.

'No. You'll be fast asleep and won't feel a thing so don't worry about that.'

He glanced round when there was a sudden commotion at the next bed. A junior doctor from the paediatric unit was kicking up a fuss because there was no one available to take his patient up to the ward. Nick frowned when he heard the young man subject the staff to a barrage of abuse. He quickly excused himself and went over to speak to him.

'You need to calm down,' he said firmly, drawing the younger man aside. 'The staff are under enough pressure as it is without you giving them any more hassle.'

The young doctor coloured angrily at the rebuke but obviously decided it would be wiser not to say anything. Nick left him to make his peace with the staff and went back to Jodie.

'Sorry about that. It's very busy today and tempers are getting a bit frayed. Anyway, I'm going to move you out of here as soon as I can but I need to speak to your mum and dad first. Do you want me to give them a message from you?'

'No.' Tears trickled down Jodie's face and she quickly turned her head away.

'Shh, it's all going to be OK. Don't upset yourself now.'

Nick gently squeezed her hand then moved away from the bed. It was obvious that the girl didn't want her parents knowing what had happened but there was no way he could avoid telling them when he was going to have to operate on her. He left Resus and made his way to the relatives' room. Mr and Mrs Carmichael were sitting side by side on the sofa and he waved them back to their seats when they jumped up.

'No, please, sit down.' He pulled up a chair and sat down, facing them. 'First of all let me assure you that Jodie is going to be fine. She needs an operation but she's in no immediate danger.'

'Oh, thank heavens for that!' Mrs Carmichael gasped. 'I didn't know what to think when I went into her bedroom and saw all that blood.'

Nick nodded. 'It must have been a shock for you, I imagine.'

'Oh, it was, wasn't it, Derek?' she said, turning to her husband.

'It was indeed. Do you know what's wrong with her, Doctor...?' Derek Carmichael paused. 'I'm sorry but I don't know your name.'

'Nick Lawson. I'm a specialist registrar on the obs and gynae unit.'

'Oh, I see. So what's happened to Jodie is some sort of female problem, is it?' Derek asked uncertainly.

'Yes, but maybe not quite what you have in mind.' Nick chose his words with care because he knew it would be a shock for the couple to learn that their daughter had had a baby. 'Jodie has recently given birth and part of the placenta has been retained inside her womb. That's what has caused all the bleeding.'

'Given birth? Is this some sort of a joke?' Derek shot to his feet. 'I've heard some rubbish in my time but this really takes the biscuit. My daughter is sixteen years old and you're trying to tell us that she's had a baby!'

'I'm sorry but it's true,' Nick replied calmly because it wouldn't achieve anything to get into an argument. Even though he couldn't understand how the parents had failed to notice their daughter was pregnant, that wasn't the issue at the moment. 'Jodie has given birth within the past forty-eight hours. I can tell that from examining her so there's no doubt at all in my mind about what's happened.'

'They found that baby on Christmas Day, didn't they? The one that was left down by the river,' Mrs Carmichael said slowly. She pressed a trembling hand to her mouth. 'That was Jodie's baby, wasn't it? She left it there because she didn't know what else to do.'

Nick sighed because he could understand how upsetting this must be for the girl's parents. 'Obviously, we'll need to carry out some tests before we can confirm that Jodie is the child's mother, but it seems very likely.'

'What do you mean, *it seems likely*? Has Jodie said that it's her baby?' Derek demanded.

'No, she hasn't. She's still refusing to admit that she's had a baby,' Nick explained.

'There you go, then. That just proves it, doesn't it?' Derek scowled at him. 'You doctors are all the same. You come up with all these fancy theories and expect folks to believe you. It's a complete load of rubbish, do you hear me? Absolute rot.'

'Stop it!' Margaret Carmichael jumped to her feet and rounded on her husband. 'If anyone's talking rubbish

it's you! I told you that I was worried about Jodie staying in her bedroom all the time, didn't I, but you just
told me to stop fussing. She was probably hiding up
there so we wouldn't notice she was pregnant! And she
was too scared to tell us what she'd done with the baby
after she'd had it because she knew how you'd react.
You're nothing but a bully, Derek, but you're not going
to bully that poor child ever again!'

She turned to Nick, ignoring her husband who was
staring at her in open-mouthed amazement. 'I'd like to
see my daughter now, Dr Lawson. I want her to know
that she isn't in any trouble. If anyone's to blame for
this then it's us for making her feel that she couldn't
tell us the truth.'

'Of course. If you'd like to come with me, Mrs
Carmichael, I'll take you to see her.' Nick glanced at
the other man. 'Would you like to come, too?'

'No, I most certainly wouldn't!'

Derek stormed out of the room, slamming the door
behind him. Nick didn't say anything but he could tell
how upset Jodie's mother was as he accompanied her
to Resus. He left mother and daughter together while
he checked that Theatre was ready for him and was
pleased to see they were holding hands when he went
back. With a bit of luck the father would come round
eventually, but at least the girl had her mother's support
and that was something.

Mrs Carmichael accompanied them in the lift to
Theatre. Nick left her in the waiting room then handed
Jodie over to the anaesthetist. Larry was having a day
off so he would be working with another member of
the team, a young woman called Mary Hopkirk.

They exchanged the usual pleasantries then Nick
went to scrub up while Mary started the premed. Jodie

was already in Theatre when he arrived so he lost no time cleaning out the debris that had been left behind in her womb. It wasn't a complicated procedure but the risk of infection was extremely high so he took meticulous care over it. Fortunately there was very little tearing from the delivery so he only needed to put in a couple of stitches and he was done.

Jodie would need antibiotics as a precautionary measure because of the high risk of infection but he was confident that she'd make a full recovery physically, at least. How she would cope with the rest was impossible to foretell, but he didn't allow himself to dwell on it as he sent the girl to Recovery then went to have a word with her mother. The one thing he'd had to learn was that he couldn't solve everyone's problems, although it wasn't always easy to detach himself. Some people just seemed to get to him more than others did. Like Katie, for instance.

Nick sighed as he opened the waiting-room door because everything kept coming back to Katie.

CHAPTER SIX

KATIE had the room ready by the time Jodie was brought down from Theatre. Following Nick's instructions, she hadn't said anything to the rest of the staff, although she would have to explain the situation to them at some point, of course. She got the girl settled then wrote up her chart, adding the time and the date when Jodie had been admitted to the unit. Nick had written her up for broad-spec. antibiotics so she double-checked that they'd been administered via the intravenous drip.

Once she was sure everything was in order she called in Abbey. She'd decided that the trainee should special Jodie because it would help to keep a lid on the gossip if there was just one member of staff responsible for her care. She quickly explained the situation to Abbey then went through Jodie's chart with her to make sure the trainee was clear about what needed doing. By the time that was finished, Nick had arrived so she left Abbey to keep an eye on the girl while she went to speak to him.

'How did it go?' she asked.

'OK. I got everything cleaned out so, hopefully, she won't go down with an infection.'

Katie frowned when she heard the rather sombre note in his voice. 'Are you worried about her?'

'No, not really.' He summoned a smile. 'I guess I'm just a bit tired, that's all.'

'No wonder. You've been working almost non-stop since you got here. Niall will be wondering if you're

87

after his job if you carry on like this,' she said lightly, although she sensed there was rather more to it than he was admitting.

'He needn't worry. I won't be here long enough to pose a threat to him.' He smiled again but she couldn't help noticing how strained he looked. She was on the point of asking him if there was anything she could do to help when the lift arrived at their floor and a woman stepped out.

'That's Jodie's mother,' Nick explained. 'Apparently, the parents had no idea she was pregnant so this has been rather a shock for them. The mother seems to be handling the situation fairly well, considering, but the father's a different story. Just be wary if he turns up, will you? He seems like the sort who could kick up a fuss.'

'Thanks for the warning.' Katie grimaced. 'Although we could do without him making a scene if we're trying to keep this quiet. I've just told Abbey what's happened so far, but I'll have to tell the rest of the staff soon. I can't keep it quiet for ever.'

'Of course not, but if we could try to keep everything low-key for a day or two then at least it will give the poor kid time to sort herself out.' His tone was grim. 'Once the press get to know they'll move heaven and earth to get hold of the story. I don't want them putting any more pressure on her.'

'They won't hear about it from us,' Katie assured him, wondering what had caused him to have such a poor opinion of the press. Did Nick have personal experience of the way they worked, perhaps?

It was impossible to answer that question and she had to set it aside when Jodie Carmichael's mother approached them. Nick introduced Katie to her then asked her if she would take Mrs Carmichael to see her daughter while he finished writing up his notes. Jodie was still a little groggy from the anaesthetic when they went into the room but Katie knew that would soon wear off. And as long as there was no sign of infection she should be fine in a few days' time. Katie wasn't sure what would happen about the baby if it did turn out to be Jodie's. It would depend on what the girl wanted to do, of course. However, as she left the room she couldn't help wishing for a happy ending for this particular story. It would be lovely to know that mother and child had been reunited but life was rarely as cut and dried as she'd like it to be.

That thought immediately brought her back to Nick and she groaned. Five whole minutes and she hadn't thought about him. It must be a record!

Katie had the next two days off and spent the first one catching up with some of the jobs that needed doing. A couple of loads of washing resulted in a stack of ironing but at least she had some clean clothes to wear afterwards.

On the second day, Mel asked her to go into town with her and they spent a pleasant couple of hours, trawling the shops. Katie tried not to get too despondent when her friend explained that Nick had promised to let her know if he could go the ball once he found out when he was supposed to be working. He obviously wanted to go to the dance, Katie realised, or he would have turned Mel down, so she told her friend that Nick wasn't rostered to work on New Year's Eve.

Mel was thrilled by the news and immediately decided that she needed something new to wear so they did a second foray through the shops. She finally found a dress she liked in one of the new boutiques that had opened in the high street then insisted that Katie must buy something as well. Katie hadn't decided if she was going to the ball. Although she'd been planning on going because a lot of her friends would be there, she wasn't sure how she'd feel on the night if she had to watch Mel and Nick dancing together. However, there was no way she could explain all that to Mel so she went along with her friend's request and ended up buying a beautiful burgundy crêpe dress because it fitted her so perfectly that she couldn't bear to put it back on the rack. Hopefully, there'd be other occasions when she could wear it if she did chicken out of going to the ball that year.

She went back into work on the Wednesday morning and found both Niall and Nick in the office when she arrived. They were looking very grim so she and Jean did the handover as quickly as possible. Jean scuttled out of the room as soon as the formalities had been completed, leaving Katie to find out for herself what had been going on.

'What's happened?' she demanded.

'Obviously, you've not seen the newspaper this morning, have you?' Niall handed her a copy of the local morning paper and Katie gasped when she saw the headline: LOCAL TEENAGER IS MOTHER OF ABANDONED CHRISTMAS BABY. She quickly skimmed through the report and was horrified to see that the reporter had given Jodie's name, age and her home address as well.

'How on earth did they get hold of all that information?' she asked in dismay.

'That's what I'd like to know, too.' Niall's expression was grim. 'I've already had Jodie's father on the phone and he's furious about what's happened. Apparently, the national press have now picked up the story and there's reporters camped outside his house. He's threatening to sue the hospital for breach of patient confidentiality and I really can't blame him. It's gross professional mis-conduct to discuss a patient with a third party and I won't tolerate such behaviour from my staff.'

'I'm sure none of our staff would talk to the press,' Katie protested. 'If the story's come from someone in-side the hospital it must be a member of staff from another department. After all, Abbey was the only per-son who knew anything about this apart from myself and Nick. We were trying to keep it quiet.'

'So I believe, which is why I want to see Abbey in my office as soon as she arrives for duty.' Niall strode to the door. 'I'd like you to be there as well, please, Katie. As her line manager, you'll need to be involved if disciplinary action is taken.'

Katie couldn't hide her dismay when Niall left the office. 'I know he's right to be concerned but I honestly don't believe that Abbey had anything to do with this leak. She isn't the sort of person who'd go around spreading gossip like that.'

'It's surprising what people will do with the right incentive,' Nick stated bluntly. 'Newspapers will pay a lot of money for a story like this and it can be very tempting to take advantage of their generosity.'

'No, I'm sorry, but Abbey would never sell infor-mation about a patient. If the leak has come from this department it will have been an accident.'

'Let's hope your faith isn't misplaced,' Nick replied flatly.

'It isn't.' She frowned. 'You seem to have a pretty

poor opinion of how people will behave. Is it based on personal experience?'

'I just have a more realistic view of the world than you do. Not everyone is as honest as you are, Katie, and you should remember that. There are people in this world who will do anything for money.'

'And these people—did they do something to you?' she asked softly because she desperately needed to know. Maybe she was reading too much into this but she sensed it could go a long way towards explaining Nick's behaviour.

'Nothing that makes any difference now.' He glanced round when there was a knock on the door. 'That must be Abbey. I'll leave you to sort this out. Niall has asked me to take clinic as he's going to be tied up for most of the morning. I'll see you later.'

'Yes.'

Katie sighed as he left and Abbey came into the office. She would have dearly loved to have made him tell her more about what had happened in his past but it wasn't the right time to worry about it. Abbey had seen the morning paper and she'd guessed that people would think she was responsible for leaking the story. However, she was adamant that she'd had nothing to do with it and Katie believed her.

They went to Niall's office and Katie backed her up as she told Niall that she had no idea who'd told the press about Jodie Carmichael being the mother of the abandoned baby. Niall obviously believed her because he apologised for doubting her, but the whole episode had left rather a cloud hanging over the department. Several of the mums had seen the article and some were up in arms about what the teenager had done. Katie calmed things down as best she could but she was in the difficult position of not being able to defend Jodie properly because she wasn't allowed to discuss the case. It was almost a relief when Rosie Meadows phoned from the antenatal clinic to say that she wasn't feeling well.

Katie told her that she'd be straight there and went to relieve her. Nick was in the consulting room and he looked up when she knocked on the door and went in. 'Thanks for coming so quickly. Poor Rosie looks as though she's coming down with that wretched flu.'

'She does. I've sent her home with strict instructions to go straight to bed.' She sighed. 'That's another one down. We seem to be dropping like flies at the moment, although I have to admit that I wasn't sorry to get away for a while. You could have cut the atmosphere upstairs with a knife.'

Nick frowned. 'That poor kid. I can imagine what the other mums are saying about her. We'll have to see if we can move her somewhere else.' He glanced at the pile of folders on his desk. 'Anyway, we'd better get started so could you ask Lucy Brothers to come in, please?'

Katie went out to the waiting room. Lucy was a new patient and this was her first visit to the clinic. Since she'd arrived, she'd given a detailed medical history, been weighed and had provided a urine sample. She'd also given a sample of blood for testing and Katie took the slip of paper containing all the details from Lucy as she showed her into the room.

Nick stood up and shook hands. 'Hello. I'm Nick Lawson, the new specialist registrar on the obs and gynae unit.'

'Pleased to meet you, Dr Lawson.' Lucy smiled as she sat down. 'This is all very new to me so I feel a bit out of my depth, I'm afraid. My head's positively spinning with all the things I've had to do so far!'

Nick laughed. 'Fed up with being poked and prodded already, are you?'

'A bit, although I'm sure I'll get used to it by the time Junior arrives,' Lucy agreed with a smile.

'I know it can seem a bit overwhelming at first but everything we do here is for a reason. We want to make sure that you and your baby are healthy,' Nick told her. He glanced at the slip of paper that Katie had placed on his desk. 'I see from this that your blood group is AB positive so that's fine. We won't have to worry about rhesus incompatibility. Your weight is also perfect for your height, although we'll keep an eye on it as your pregnancy advances, of course.'

'How much weight are you allowed to gain?' Lucy interjected. She chuckled. 'My mum keeps telling me that she put on four stone when she was having me and at that rate I'll end up looking like the side of a house!'

Nick laughed. 'We'll certainly try and keep you under the four-stone mark. It isn't good for you or the baby if you carry that much extra weight around. Twelve and a half kilos—that's roughly two stone—is the maximum we normally recommend.'

'I'll remember that,' Lucy agreed. 'Not too many cream cakes and pickles from now on.'

'Already getting cravings, are you?' Nick asked lightly, drawing over the file and reading through the patient's history.

'I think I must be. I've never really liked pickled onions that much but I've eaten a whole jar all by myself this week.' She laughed. 'My husband says that kissing me now is a whole new experience.'

'I can imagine.' Nick smiled but Katie could tell that

Because the placenta has the same genetic make-up as the baby, we can check for any chromosomal problems. The other advantage of CVS is that the test can be done quite early in the pregnancy, between nine and twelve weeks, in fact.'

'It's a lot to take in,' Lucy admitted. 'I have to confess that I never even considered the possibility that because Tim's brother has cystic fibrosis there might be a risk that our baby has it.'

'It's a very slight risk,' Nick assured her. 'I'm sure your baby will be fine but I wanted you to know that there are tests available if you should choose to have them done. So now that we've got that all covered, I'd like to examine you. Can you take over, please, Sister?'

'Of course.'

Katie took Lucy behind the screen and helped her into a gown then waited while Nick carried out a basic internal examination to check that everything was as it should be. Lucy got dressed again then told them that she'd decided she would like to be screened for cystic fibrosis so Nick wrote out a note for the lab and sent her back to the admissions nurse to have another blood sample taken.

He sighed as the door closed behind her. 'She must be sorry now that she mentioned her brother-in-law. It's rather taken the shine off her first antenatal visit, hasn't it?'

'Best to be safe,' Katie said firmly. 'If you suspect there might be a problem it would be silly not to do something about it, wouldn't it?'

'Yes, it would.'

There was the oddest note in Nick's voice and Katie felt the hair on the back on her neck lift. She knew he wasn't thinking about Lucy Brothers at that moment and had to bite her lip to hold back the question that was dying to get out. Nick was thinking about some other problem, and why did she have the feeling that it had something to do with her?

Unfortunately, there was no opportunity to ask Nick anything more because they were too busy. They saw the rest of the patients who were booked into the clinic that day then Katie went back to the maternity unit and found the place in a state of chaos. It appeared that the press had been phoning almost non-stop while she'd been away, asking for information about Jodie, and the staff had been under tremendous pressure trying to cope.

Katie contacted the switchboard and told them not to put through any more calls to the department. All calls should be directed to her office and she would deal with them from now on. It helped to calm things down but the staff were obviously unsettled by what was happening and it didn't help when one of the reporters tried to sneak into the unit by posing as a visitor.

Katie called Security and had the man escorted from the building but she knew they couldn't continue that way. It felt as though they were under siege and it wasn't fair to the patients or the staff. The least affected by it all seemed to be Jodie because she was tucked away in a side room and had no idea what was happening. Katie went to see her and was pleased to discover that the girl looked a lot better than she'd done when she'd been admitted.

'Your temperature is fine,' Katie told her, checking the girl's chart. 'That's a good indication there's no infection brewing, but how do you feel?'

'A bit sore—down there,' Jodie told her shyly.

She was a pretty girl with long dark brown hair and looked far younger than her sixteen years. Katie couldn't help wondering how she'd managed to get herself into this predicament in the first place, but it wasn't her place to ask. The police had phoned to say that they wanted to interview Jodie as soon as she was well enough to speak to them, and Social Services would need to get involved at some point. The poor girl would have enough people asking her questions so Katie hung the chart on the end of the bed and smiled at her.

'You're bound to experience a bit of discomfort for a few days but it will soon clear up. I'll ask Abbey to help you take a salt bath. You'll find it very soothing. I'll send her in to you in a few minutes.'

'Thank you,' the girl said quietly.

'You're welcome.' Katie left the room and almost bumped right into Jodie's mother. It was obvious the woman was upset so Katie drew her into an alcove so they could talk in private.

'I was just getting myself a cup of coffee from the machine and I heard one of the nurses saying that there's been reporters phoning up about Jodie,' the woman explained anxiously. 'Is it true, Sister?'

'I'm afraid so.' Katie sighed. 'We even had one fellow try to sneak in here by posing as a visitor.'

'Oh, no!' Mrs Carmichael looked stricken. 'I don't want poor Jodie to find out what's been going on. She's got enough to deal with without all this as well.'

'She won't hear about it from us,' Katie assured her. 'I know your husband seems to believe that one of the maternity unit staff leaked the story to the press, but I know for a fact that the people who work in this department would never do such a thing.'

'I'm sure you're right,' Mrs Carmichael said hurriedly, looking embarrassed. 'Derek's biggest problem is that he won't listen. He has such set ideas about everything and always thinks he's right. Anyway, I'd be really grateful, Sister, if you could ask the staff not to let Jodie see any of those newspapers. I've read what they're saying about her and it's horrible. I don't want her getting upset.'

'Don't worry. I'll make sure everyone keeps the papers well away from her. But she's bound to find out what's been going on at some point, you do realise?'

'I know that but I just want to…well, protect her for as long as I can.' Tears welled into the woman's eyes. 'It's the least I can do. I'll never forgive myself because she felt she couldn't confide in me.'

Katie sighed as Mrs Carmichael hurried back to her daughter, wishing there was some way to make the situation easier for them both. She decided that the only thing she could do was to protect Jodie's privacy and make sure the girl didn't see all the awful things that were being written about her so she gathered the staff together and explained that Jodie mustn't be given any newspapers then reminded them not to talk about the case outside the maternity unit.

Everyone promised to be careful so Katie left it at that. There wasn't much else she could do, in all honesty, but she decided to have a word with Nick and see if he had any ideas about how to protect the girl from any more unwanted attention. He arrived half an hour later so Katie asked him to come to the office after he'd seen Jodie and explained what had happened when he got there.

'I'm not sure what to suggest for the best,' he said worriedly. 'I had been thinking about moving Jodie because of the other mums, but I'm no longer sure if it would be a good idea. At least the press can't get to her here because we screen all the visitors coming into the unit.' He grimaced. 'It doesn't help you very much, though. Can you cope with the continued disruption if we leave her here?'

'We'll have to,' Katie said firmly. 'There's no way I'm throwing that poor kid to the lions!'

Nick laughed. 'Good for you. Anyway, the good news is that Jodie's finally admitted that baby you found is hers. She's asked to see him so I'm going to check with SCBU to see how he's doing then make all the arrangements.

'Apparently, the child's father is a boy she met on an exchange visit to France, arranged by her school. She doesn't intend to see him again but her mother has told her that she will help look after the child if Jodie wants to take him home.'

'Oh, that's brilliant!' Katie declared. 'I was hoping for a happy ending.'

Nick shook his head. 'Now, don't get too excited. There's a long way to go yet. Social Services will want to check that she understands what she's taking on and—'

'And nothing! You've just said that Jodie's mum has offered to help her look after the baby so of course she'll be able to manage.'

'Let's hope so.' Nick glanced at his watch. 'I'd better dash. I promised Niall that I'd bring him up to speed about what's been happening over Christmas. He's not had much chance to catch up with all the fuss that's been going on today.'

'Well, make sure you tell him that we couldn't have coped without you,' Katie said sternly. 'No hiding your light under a bushel.'

'As I have no idea what a bushel is, I might find it rather difficult.'

'Never mind changing the subject, Nick Lawson. If you don't tell Niall what a star you've been then I shall.'

'I was only doing my job, Katie,' he said quietly, his expression turning sombre all of a sudden.

She shook her head. 'You did a lot more than that, Nick.'

His hazel eyes filled with sudden warmth and he smiled at her. 'Then thank you. That means a lot to me, Katie.'

'You're very welcome,' she murmured as he hurried away. She took a deep breath but it was impossible to ignore the fact that, little by little, her feelings for Nick were growing deeper. She couldn't help feeling scared by what was happening because she had no idea where it was going to lead. Nick was only going to be in Dalverston for a few months and she didn't want to start hoping that he would stay longer when there was no basis for it. Her heart lurched because, sensible or not, she knew there was going to be a big gap in her life when Nick left.

The rest of the shift flew past with barely a minute to spare. Lara Henderson and her baby were well enough to be discharged so Katie helped get the baby ready. Once he was dressed, she wrapped him in a cosy fleece blanket and strapped him securely into the carrying chair that Lara's boyfriend had brought with him.

'All ready to go home now, poppet,' she said, stroking the infant's soft little cheek. 'Have you decided on a name for him yet?'

'Stephen,' Lara told her with a smile. 'It's my dad's

name and he's absolutely thrilled to bits because we're naming the baby after him.'

'Lovely idea,' Katie told her warmly. 'Now, don't forget that if you're at all worried just give us a call. It can be a bit scary at first looking after a new baby so don't feel that you have to manage all by yourself. And, of course, your health visitor will be in contact very shortly so she'll be on hand to give you any advice you may need.'

'I'll remember. Thank you so much for everything you've done. And will you thank Dr Lawson for us as well?' Lara sighed as she looked at her small son. 'Things might not have turned out so well if it weren't for him.'

Katie accompanied the young couple to the door and waved them off then went back inside. There were just a couple of hours of her shift left and before she knew it, it was time to go off duty. She handed over to Jean then fetched her coat and headed for the lift. She was just about to step inside it when she spotted Nick hurrying along the corridor so she held the door open for him.

'This is getting to be a habit. You're always opening doors for me!'

'At least I come in useful for something,' Katie joked, trying to keep the mood light because she didn't want Nick to get any inkling of what she'd been thinking earlier that day. Maybe she would miss him when he left but he wasn't leaving for a while yet so there was no point worrying about it. Anyway, she didn't want to make the mistake she'd made with David by getting too involved, too quickly, did she?

She felt a little easier after that and chatted about what had happened during the day as the lift carried them down to the ground floor. She was just passing along Lara Henderson's thanks when they stepped out into the foyer and she stopped when she saw the crowd of people milling about.

'What on earth is going on?'

'Looks like the press,' Nick replied grimly. 'They're probably after more information about Jodie.'

He took her arm and steered her through the crush of people, shaking his head when a reporter pushed a microphone into his face and demanded to know if he worked there. Katie heaved a sigh of relief when they finally made it out of the main doors.

'It's absolute bedlam. I wonder why Security haven't moved them out of the building.'

'They probably will as soon as they can muster enough staff,' Nick told her. 'I had a word with the head of security about that reporter who managed to sneak into the maternity unit and he told me that this flu epidemic has hit them hard. Apparently, they've been struggling to cover all the shifts.'

'Typical it should happen now, isn't it?' Katie said wryly, leading the way round the side of the building. She ground to a halt when she spotted the crowd gathered around the entrance to the staff block, causing Nick to cannon into her back.

'Sorry,' she said, glancing at him. 'But it looks as though the press have set up camp outside the staff residence as well.'

'That's all we need, isn't it? Is there another way in, do you know?'

'No. There's just the fire doors but you can only open them from the inside.' She looked back towards the way they'd come. 'Maybe we could get one of the security staff over here to move them away?'

'I expect Security will have enough to do, clearing the hospital. No, it looks like it's time for plan B.'

'Plan B. What's that?'

'That we take the easy option and go to the pub for something to eat.' He grinned at her. 'With a bit of luck those reporters will get fed up standing around in the cold and have gone home by the time we come back so how about it?'

Katie took a deep breath. She knew what her answer should be, of course. Hadn't she just admitted that her feelings for Nick were growing too intense too quickly? It would be silly to make matters worse by spending the evening with him. She opened her mouth to tell him that she was too tired to go out only the words came out rather different from what she'd planned.

'Sounds good to me!'

CHAPTER SEVEN

'ONE glass of red wine, as requested. And the waitress said to tell you that our food will be ready in about fifteen minutes' time.'

Nick put the glasses on the table, hoping Katie couldn't tell how nervous he felt. Asking her out must come under the same heading as that near-miss he'd had in the kitchen the other day—a *huge* mistake. He certainly hadn't been planning on inviting her to spend the evening with him—it had just happened. Now he would have to deal with it the best way he could so he picked up his glass after he'd sat down.

'How about a toast? May all those reporters end up with chilblains for their efforts!'

'I'll second that!' Katie clinked her glass against his then took a sip of her wine. 'Mmm, that's nice. Definitely better than your average pub wine.'

'Good. Some of it can taste like vinegar, which is why I usually stick to good old-fashioned beer.' He took a swallow of his drink and sighed ecstatically, deliberately hamming things up because he wanted to keep the mood light. 'Delicious even if it is shandy rather than the pure stuff.'

'Well, it may be delicious but I don't think you actually wanted a beer moustache, did you?'

Katie leant across the table and wiped a smidgen of froth off his upper lip and Nick almost leapt right out of his seat. He set his glass on a coaster but his heart was pounding and various other bits of his anatomy were doing things he didn't dare think about. Taking a handkerchief out of his pocket, he carefully wiped his mouth, trying not to think about how cool Katie's fingers had felt when they'd touched him. It was best not to go down that route and definitely safer not to wonder how they'd feel on other parts of his body…

Nick groaned under his breath because, predictably, he now couldn't think of anything else. Katie's fingers would be so cool as they stroked him and he ached to feel them caressing him, but he had to be sensible and not forget those rules he'd made. He mustn't do anything that might hurt Katie and if that meant *him* suffering then it would be worth it.

'Are you OK?'

He looked up, feeling his stomach lurch when he saw the concern in her eyes. 'I'm fine,' he assured her robustly, hoping that he might be able to convince himself as well as her. 'I'm just hungry. I never had time for any lunch today and my stomach is complaining.'

'Oh, I see. I thought you looked a bit distracted.'

She laughed and Nick smiled because there wasn't much else he could do. Keep it light, Lawson, he reminded himself sternly, be witty and amusing and everything will be fine. He picked up his glass again as he hunted for something to say, but Katie beat him to it.

'It's been ages since I last came here. It's a bit of a trek from the hospital so we tend to use the pubs along the by-pass if we go out for a drink after work. This makes a very pleasant change.'

'I thought it might be better if we went further afield,' Nick explained, gratefully latching onto the new topic. 'Those reporters have probably got the local pubs staked out in the hope they'll find someone from the hospital willing to talk to them.'

'I doubt they'll get much joy. Most of the staff probably feel the same way we do and won't want to talk to the press.'

'Let's hope so,' Nick agreed, wishing he could be as sure of that as she was. As he knew to his cost, the lure of talking to the press often overruled a person's scruples.

Katie put down her glass and looked at him. 'Look, Nick, tell me to mind my own business if you like, but did the press ever cause you a problem?' She shrugged when he didn't reply. 'You have this really funny tone in your voice whenever you mention the press and it makes me wonder if something happened to you personally.'

Nick stared into his glass, wondering how to answer the question. He never spoke about Mike's accident and the trouble it had caused because it was too painful, yet he didn't want to lie to Katie. Maybe he could give her an edited version of events?

'My experience of the press goes back to when my brother was killed a few years ago,' he said quietly. 'I don't want to go into detail. Suffice to say that the press made our lives hell.'

'Oh, I'm so sorry, Nick! I had no idea. I wish I hadn't said anything now. I certainly didn't want to go raking up a lot of bad memories for you.'

Nick sighed when he heard the guilt in her voice because he couldn't bear to hear her blaming herself when there was no need. 'It's not your fault, Katie. You weren't to know what happened, were you?'

'No, but—'

'No buts. You have nothing to be sorry for. OK?'

'OK,' she repeated obediently, but he could tell that she was upset even though she did her best not to show it.

Fortunately, their meal arrived a few minutes later so in the general confusion of handing round silverware and condiments the subject was dropped. Nick knew he should be relieved to have got off so lightly but, perversely, he found himself wishing that he'd told Katie the whole story while he'd had the chance. Maybe she could have helped him deal with these feelings of guilt that had haunted him all these years? If Katie told him that he had nothing to blame himself for it would make a world of difference. Even though it scared him to admit it, her opinion really mattered to him.

The conversation had put a bit of a dampener on the evening and Katie found it difficult to behave as though nothing was wrong when she felt so bad about upsetting Nick. She did her best to keep the conversation flowing but she was glad when Nick suggested that they should go back to the hospital as soon as they'd finished their meal. She followed him out of the pub, waiting by the car while he hunted through his pockets for his keys.

'I wonder if they fell out of your pocket when you took your coat off,' she suggested when a second search failed to find them.

'They could have done, I suppose. D'you want to hang on here while I go back and check?'

'Sure. No problem.'

Katie pulled up her coat collar as Nick sprinted back to the pub. It was a cold night and she shivered when an icy breeze blew across the car park. There were a lot of cars parked there and she looked round when another car pulled into an empty space close to where she was standing. As Katie watched, she saw a man get out and walk towards the pub and she frowned when she realised that it was the reporter who'd tried to sneak into the maternity unit that afternoon. What was he doing here?

The question had just crossed her mind when a taxi turned into the car park. It stopped outside the pub and she gasped when she saw Gary Hutchins, the junior registrar on Paediatrics, climb out. He went straight over to the reporter and said something to him then they both went inside together.

Katie could barely contain her impatience as she waited for Nick to come back. She had a feeling that she might have solved the mystery about who had been responsible for revealing that information about Jodie Carmichael to the press. She hurried across the car park when she saw Nick coming out of the door.

'Sorry to keep you waiting,' he said, misinterpreting her eagerness to speak to him. 'Someone had found the keys and handed them to the barman for safe-keeping.'

'Did you see who just went into the pub?' she demanded, grabbing hold of his arm.

'No. Why? What's wrong?'

'I just saw Gary Hutchins with that reporter who tried to worm his way into Maternity this afternoon.'

'Who's Gary Hutchins?' Nick asked, frowning.

'He's the junior reg on Paeds and a really nasty piece of work from what I can gather.'

'Really?' Nick's expression was grim as he looked back at the pub. 'There was a junior reg from Paeds in Resus when Jodie Carmichael was admitted. I remember him because he was giving the staff such a hard time.'

'Then it must be him who's been speaking to the

press!' Katie exclaimed. 'He probably saw you with Jodie and put two and two together.'

'It sounds highly likely. He could have got her details from the admissions form. It was bedlam in there, with people coming and going all the time so nobody would have thought anything of it if he'd checked her notes.' Nick swore softly. 'Damn! It was all written down just ready for Hutchins to copy out.'

'So you really think he could be the culprit?' Katie demanded eagerly. 'I mean, it has to be someone from inside the hospital who's been passing on that information to the press. Nobody else could have got hold of the details they've published.'

'I'd lay odds on it being him. That being the case, I'd like to know what's going on at this very moment.' Nick's tone was grim. 'If Hutchins has arranged to meet that reporter here, it probably means that he's got more information for him.'

'Oh, of course!' Katie exclaimed in horror.

She hastily followed Nick back into the pub and spotted Gary and the reporter sitting at a table in the corner. They were deep in conversation and her heart sank because it was obvious that the young registrar was telling the other man something of interest.

'I want to find out what's going on,' Nick said flatly. 'There's no way that pair is going to cause any more trouble for that poor kid.'

'I'm coming with you,' Katie said hurriedly. She was worried what Nick might do if their suspicions proved to be correct. It was obvious that he was in no mood to compromise and she really couldn't blame him.

They made their way through the crowd that had gathered round the bar and went to the table. Gary was so busy talking that he never noticed them until they were standing beside him. Katie saw the colour leach from his face when he suddenly looked up.

'What do you want?' he demanded.

'What do you think?' Nick said quietly but with such menace that Katie heard the younger man gulp. 'It's you who's been passing all that information to the press, isn't it, Hutchins?'

'I don't know what you're talking about,' Hutchins blustered. 'Who the hell do you think you are, accusing me like that?'

'You probably got the details off the admissions form,' Nick continued, without letting him finish. 'The fact that it was privileged information didn't matter a jot to you. All you were interested in was the money. What did they pay you for it? I hope it was enough to live on because once the powers that be find out what you've been up to you'll be looking for a new job.'

'Are you threatening me?' Hutchins demanded, his face turning livid with anger.

Nick shook his head. 'No. I don't make threats. If I say I'm going to do something I do it.' He glanced at the reporter and Katie shivered when she saw the contempt on his face. 'I don't know what our friend here has told you tonight but I'd be very careful what I printed if I were you.'

He swung round, placing his hand under Katie's elbow as he led her away from the table. Katie could feel herself trembling as they left the pub and went back to the car. The whole experience had shocked her so much that she felt positively sickened by it all. Nick didn't say a word as they drove back to the hospital and she guessed that he felt as bad as she did about what had happened. They parked in the staff area and Nick switched off the engine then turned to her.

'Are you all right?'

'Just about.' She gave a wobbly laugh then bit her lip when she felt tears sting her eyes.

Nick sighed as he reached over and pulled her into his arms. 'I'm only sorry you had to witness that, Katie. It was horrible. No wonder you're upset.'

He gently smoothed her hair back from her cheek. Katie knew that he was only trying to comfort her but the touch of his hand on her skin had unleashed a host of emotions she simply wasn't prepared for. She could feel her cheek tingling and the feeling seemed to be spreading through her entire body so that every cell and every nerve were suddenly aware of him in a way she'd never been aware of anyone before.

She gave a soft murmur and saw his eyes darken when he realised what was happening. She was actually holding her breath as she stared up at him because she had no idea what was going to happen next. And then his head started to dip and she closed her eyes because it would be just too much to look at him while he kissed her.

His lips touched hers so softly, so gently that she shivered. She could feel their coolness yet the moment their mouths met, a wave of heat enveloped her. Katie murmured in delight as Nick's lips settled more firmly onto hers. There was nothing rushed or urgent about the kiss but maybe that was what made it so seductive. Hunger and passion had their place, of course, and she didn't deny that she hoped both would come later. But this slow, tender caress made her feel so wonderfully cherished. Her heart swelled with happiness because Nick obviously wanted to take his time and savour this kiss…

'I'm sorry, Katie. I shouldn't have done that.'

Nick let her go so fast that Katie's head reeled with shock. She stared at him in confusion, trying to work out what was going on. One minute he'd been kissing her with a wealth of emotion and the next…

He ran a trembling hand over his face and her heart seemed to shrivel up when she saw the remorse in his eyes. She didn't need to hear what he had to say because she could tell just by looking at him how much he regretted what had happened.

'I didn't mean to take advantage of you like that,' he said hoarsely. 'I apologise.'

'It doesn't matter,' she whispered, her mouth trembling from the effort of forming the words. 'It was just one of those spur-of-the-moment things, I expect, so don't beat yourself up about it.'

'Thanks.' He gave her a tight smile then opened the car door. 'I'll walk you back to make sure those reporters have left then go and phone Niall. He needs to know what's happened tonight.'

Katie didn't say another word as she got out of the car. She couldn't. The feeling of disappointment that filled her was so enormous that she could barely breathe as they walked up the path together but pride dictated that she mustn't let Nick see how devastated she felt. There was nobody about when they reached the staff block so Nick just waited while she let herself in then left.

Katie went straight to her room and sat down on the bed. She didn't bother switching on the light because it demanded too much effort. Anyway, she didn't need the light on to see the truth because she could see it just as clearly in the dark.

Nick didn't feel the same about her as she did about him. Oh, maybe he felt *something*, but it wasn't what

she felt. It couldn't be because he could never have
kissed her like that then let her go, and realising it was
like rubbing salt into an open wound. She'd sworn she
wouldn't get involved with Nick too quickly but it was
already too late to prevent what was happening. She
could pretend, of course, but what would be the point
of doing that? It wouldn't alter the fact that she cared
for Nick in a way that she'd cared for no man before,
including David.

She bit her lip as panic overwhelmed her. Despite her
resolve to be sensible, she knew that she was on the
verge of falling in love with Nick and the enormity of
what was happening scared her. How awful it would be
to fall in love with a man who might never love her in
return.

'Yes, that's fine. Thanks, Niall. I'll write a full report
about what happened tonight and have it ready for you
in the morning.'

Nick put the phone back on its rest and swiftly left
the office. He made his way to the stairs, relieved when
he didn't meet anyone along the way because he really
didn't feel like being sociable. That episode with Katie
had left him feeling completely drained. Now all he
wanted was to find somewhere quiet where he could sit
and think about what he was going to do.

The residents' lounge on the second floor was empty
so he went in there and made himself a cup of coffee.
He checked his watch as he sat down, hoping that nobody would come in and interrupt him. He could have
gone back to his room, of course, but he didn't trust
himself to do that just yet. Knowing that Katie was on
the floor below him would have tested his resolve to its

limit. He had to stay away from her but it was going to be the hardest thing he'd ever had to do after tonight.

Nick groaned as he recalled the expression on her face when she'd got out of the car. It didn't take a genius to work out that he'd hurt her and it was the last thing he'd wanted to do. It was just that he'd known what would happen if he'd carried on kissing her, as she'd been expecting him to do. One kiss would never have been enough, would it? He'd have wanted two, three—a dozen even—and it wouldn't have stopped there. Once he'd savoured her mouth he'd have wanted her in his bed, her body sweet and pliant under his, her eyes filled with that warmth that made him feel as though miracles could happen.

He'd have wanted to make love to her, to fill her body with his and her head with promises of undying devotion, but he didn't have the right to do that. He had forfeited his right to love and happiness with a woman like Katie, who could fill his every waking hour with joy, when Mike had died. What right did *he* have to enjoy all those things when his brother was dead?

Anger and frustration washed over him and Nick got to his feet. He needed to focus on something other than his own problems if he was to get through this night. Someone had left a notepad on the coffee-table so he tore off a few sheets of paper and sat down at the desk. He would make a start on that report which Niall needed, jot down all the facts first to make sure he didn't miss anything out, then go back to the office and type it up. Hopefully, something good would come from this night after all.

As for Katie, he would just have to make sure that he didn't put himself in the position of being tested again. Katie must be strictly off limits from now on. He would be polite and courteous to her at work but that was as far as it would go. There certainly mustn't be any more outings to the pub! Katie deserved so much more than he could give her even if his heart did shrivel up at the thought of her finding happiness with anyone else.

CHAPTER EIGHT

KATIE was working from six till two the following day so she was already in the delivery suite when Abbey came to tell her that Niall wanted to speak to her. She knew it must be important if he'd asked to speak to her when she was with a patient so she excused herself and hurried to the office. Nick was there when she arrived as well as Martin Hopkins, the hospital's manager, and another man whom she didn't recognise. It was obvious that something really serious had happened from the expressions on their faces and she couldn't help feeling alarmed as she went into the room.

'I'm sorry to drag you away from your patient, Katie. However, I'm afraid there's been some very serious allegations made about this department.' Niall's tone was clipped and Katie could tell that he was furiously angry.

'Have they anything to do with Jodie Carmichael?' she queried, glancing from him to Nick, who looked equally angry.

'Yes. You probably haven't seen the paper this morning because you're on the early shift.'

Niall handed her a newspaper and her heart sank when she saw the photograph of Jodie that was plastered across the front page. The girl was lying in bed, asleep, and what made it worse was the fact that the picture could only have been taken inside the maternity unit. Katie recognised the bed linen so there was no doubt in her mind about the location.

'How on earth did the press get hold of a picture like this?' she exclaimed.

'That's what we'd like to know, too,' Martin Hopkins said curtly. 'It could only have been taken by a member of staff because nobody else had access to the girl's room. I've spoken to Jodie's mother and she told me that she'd spent the day here with her. However, she also pointed out that she'd popped out a couple of times for coffee or a snack so the photograph must have been taken while she was out of the room. Obviously, somebody was keeping track of her movements.'

'Maybe that's why Gary Hutchins had arranged to meet that reporter last night,' Katie said slowly. She turned to Nick, hoping that he couldn't tell how hard it was for her to behave as though nothing had happened between them the previous night. 'Did you notice if he had any photographs with him?'

Nick shook his head. 'I didn't see any sign of them but that doesn't mean he isn't responsible for taking this photo. It would be just the sort of thing he'd do, in my opinion.'

'My client denies all responsibility for the photograph and whatever else has been printed in the newspapers recently.'

Katie glanced round when the other man suddenly interrupted their conversation. As she watched, he took a typewritten sheet out of his briefcase and handed it to Martin Hopkins.

'As you can see from this, Dr Hutchins has made a statement to the effect that the sole reason he agreed to meet that reporter last night was because he was so concerned about what has been happening recently. He was hoping that he might be able to persuade him not to publish anything else.'

'And you really expect us to believe that?' Katie demanded, not even bothering to hide her disdain.

'I think it would be very unwise of you to cast doubts on its veracity, Miss Denning.' The man looked coldly at her. 'My client is extremely anxious to protect his good name and he won't hesitate to seek recompense from anyone who slanders him.' He turned to Martin Hopkins again. 'I don't imagine the board of trustees would appreciate being involved in an expensive law suit either.'

'Certainly not,' said Martin Hopkins. 'The board will, naturally, take a very firm stance on this matter and it will be fully investigated. Meanwhile, any member of staff who is found to be spreading malicious rumours will face disciplinary action.'

The two men left a short time later. Niall's face was grim as he tossed the newspaper into the bin. 'It looks as though Hutchins is going to get away with it, doesn't it? The last thing I want is anyone from this department getting entangled in a messy law suit. What's happened is bad enough. The reputation of this whole department is hanging in the balance after recent events.'

'It makes me sick to think of Hutchins getting off scot-free after the trouble he's caused,' Nick said harshly. 'I can't believe that anyone would sink so low as to take a photograph of that poor kid while she was in here!'

'But when did he manage to take it?' Katie asked worriedly. 'I know Mrs Carmichael wasn't in the room with Jodie all day long but surely we'd have noticed if Hutchins had tried to sneak in there.'

'Maybe he did it when you were dealing with that reporter,' Niall suggested. 'They could have worked it together so that one created a diversion while the other took the pictures.'

'I doubt if they'd have needed to go to those lengths,' Nick pointed out. 'After all, nobody would have thought it strange to see a member of staff from another department up here. Staff have free run of the place so Hutchins could have slipped in at any point during the day.'

'He could,' Katie conceded. 'I can always ask if anyone saw him, I suppose, but it won't make much difference even if they did. It's not *proof* that he took the photograph and he's bound to dispute it was him. Hutchins seems to have covered all the angles, doesn't he?'

'He might think he has but he'll slip up at some point and we'll be ready for him when he does,' Niall said grimly, picking up the phone. 'I'll have a word with Mark Dawson, the head of Paediatrics, and tell him what's happened. Maybe he can keep an eye on young Dr Hutchins.'

'Actually, I was meaning to ask you to speak to Mark about him,' Katie said, quickly relaying what Mel had told her about Hutchins. 'He's a really nasty piece of work, isn't he?' she concluded.

'He is indeed. Unfortunately, unless Mel is prepared to make a formal complaint about his actions there isn't anything we can do about it. But he'll get his comeuppance at some point, you can be sure of that,' Niall said firmly.

Katie could only hope he was right because it didn't seem fair that Hutchins should get away with what he'd done. She left the office, glancing round when she realised that Nick had followed her out. 'Let's just hope that Niall can do something,' she said as they walked along the corridor together. She summoned a smile, because she was determined not to make things difficult when they had to work together. 'It wouldn't be fair if the bad guy won, would it?'

'No, it wouldn't, but life isn't fair, I'm afraid. It certainly isn't fair on poor Jodie to have her photo splashed across the front of the newspaper like that.'

'Hopefully, she won't see it,' Katie said soothingly because she could tell how angry he was. 'We managed to keep the papers away from her when the news first broke so we'll just have to do the same thing this time.'

'She's going to find out at some point,' Nick stated bluntly. 'Things like this have a nasty habit of coming out and I doubt if her mother will be able to shield her from it for ever.'

'Then maybe it would be better if she was told what's been going on,' Katie suggested. 'That way it will be less of a shock for her when she leaves here. I mean, someone is bound to mention it when she goes home.'

'You could be right.' Nick frowned as he considered the idea. 'Even if her friends don't mention it, the press aren't just going to let the story drop. They're probably still camped outside the Carmichaels' home so Jodie is bound to find out what's been going on when she's discharged from here. It might be easier for her and her family if she was warned in advance.'

'You could have a word with her mother and see how she feels about the idea.'

'I think I will. Mind you, I'm not sure if Mrs Carmichael will listen to anything I have to say after this latest episode.' His voice grated. 'Her faith in this department and the staff who work here must have hit rock-bottom by now. And the worst thing is that the person responsible isn't the one who's going to have to carry the can.'

Katie sighed as they parted company. Nick had every right to be angry because it wasn't fair that Hutchins's actions should have such a detrimental effect on the reputation of the department. They all worked extremely hard to maintain high standards of care, but their patients' trust was vital if they were to work successfully together. She guessed that a lot of their mums would be unsettled by what had happened so all they could do was to reassure them that nothing like it would happen in the future. It wasn't going to be easy, though, because once people lost faith it was difficult to make them trust you again.

Did Nick trust her? she suddenly wondered. He'd told her a little about what had happened in his past but she knew there was a lot more that he'd held back. However, the fact that he'd been let down could explain why he was so wary of getting involved with anyone.

She sighed because even if they couldn't be anything more than friends, she would like to think that Nick trusted her, but maybe even that was hoping for too much.

'Try to work with the next contraction, Jessica. When you feel it starting *then* you can push... Good. That's great.'

Katie smiled at the exhausted young woman on the bed but she couldn't help feeling worried when she checked the time on the clock. Jessica Morris had been making very slow progress since she'd been admitted that morning. Although labour had started spontaneously, it hadn't continued so Jessica was being given intravenous synthetic oxytocin—a uterine stimulant—to help strengthen her contractions, but even that hadn't achieved very much. Katie was becoming increasingly concerned because Jessica had a history of high blood pressure throughout her pregnancy. Although labour could continue for much longer than this in normal circumstances, she didn't want to take any risks in this particular case. She checked the monitor and frowned when she saw that Jessica's blood pressure had risen slightly.

'How much longer is it going to take?' Jessica whispered weakly.

'I'm not sure but you're getting very tired, aren't you?' Katie asked, bending over her.

'I knew it was going to take a while but I didn't realise just how hard it was going to be. I just wish my husband was here but he's stuck in Paris because his flight's been cancelled.' She broke off as another contraction began.

Katie talked her through it, all the time checking to see how things were progressing. She sighed when she realised that the baby's head still wasn't crowning and turned to Abbey, who was assisting her. 'I'm going to page Niall and ask him to take a look at her. I'm not happy with her blood pressure.'

'Me neither,' Abbey agreed, checking the monitor. 'I don't think it's safe to leave her much longer, do you?'

'No. I don't.'

Katie hurried to the phone and dialled Niall's office but there was no answer. She got straight onto the switchboard next and asked the operator to page him. She'd barely got back to the bed when the door opened and Nick appeared.

'Niall's been called into a meeting with Martin Hopkins and some members of the board so his calls are being transferred to me,' he explained as he came over to her.

'No need to ask what's going on,' Katie said. 'The sooner this is all sorted out the better. Maybe then we can concentrate on what we're here for.'

'Amen to that,' he agreed, then turned to Jessica and smiled. 'Hi, I'm Nick Lawson, the new registrar on the unit. How are you doing?'

'I've had better days,' Jessica murmured drolly.

'I bet you have!' Nick laughed before he drew Katie aside so they could talk in private. 'What's the story here?'

'Jessica's been in labour for seven hours but she doesn't seem to be making much progress, I'm afraid. Her labour started spontaneously before she was admitted and when everything slowed down, we put her on oxytocin. Normally, I'd suggest that we wait a bit longer then use the ventouse to help things along. Some babies just need that extra bit of encouragement when Mum's getting tired and the suction method is so safe that normally I'm happy to use it. However, Jessica has had high blood pressure throughout her pregnancy and I'm not happy about the fact that her BP has risen in the last few minutes.'

'Is she still having good, strong contractions?' Nick asked, frowning as he considered what she'd told him so far.

'Yes. As you know, oxytocin strengthens the contractions so that isn't the problem. Basically, she's just too exhausted now to push and I'm worried about letting her carry on when her BP is playing up.'

'In that case I think the safest thing is to whiz her off to Theatre for a section,' Nick decided. 'If you're not happy with her that's good enough for me.'

Katie grinned, feeling her heart lift all of a sudden. 'So you trust my judgement, do you?'

'I most certainly do.'

He smiled at her and Katie bit her lip when she saw the warmth in his eyes. It was only a smile, she told herself sternly, and it would be foolish to start reading anything into it after last night. However, not even those sensible words could dampen her spirits.

'I'll just check her over then give Theatre a call and let them know we're on our way.' Nick glanced at the clock. 'You're supposed to be off duty, aren't you, so maybe Abbey could assist me? There's no point you hanging around and it would be good experience for her.'

'I…um…no, of course not. I'll let her know what's happening,' Katie agreed, hoping he couldn't hear the despondency in her voice.

She quickly informed a delighted Abbey that Nick wanted her to assist him in Theatre then waited while he examined Jessica and explained that they'd decided a Caesarean section would be safer for her and the baby. The young mother readily agreed and looked relieved as she signed the consent form giving them permission to go ahead. Five minutes later, Nick and Abbey were wheeling her out of the delivery room and that was that: Katie was free to leave. However, as the door closed, she couldn't pretend that she wasn't hurt by the fact that Nick hadn't wanted her to assist him that day. Had it been a deliberate decision on his part to keep her at a distance after what had happened last night?

She sensed it was so and what made the situation so much worse was that there wasn't a thing she could do about it.

*   *   *

The baby was a little girl, six pounds two ounces and perfectly healthy. Nick handed her to Abbey, trying not to think about how much he'd missed not having Katie working alongside him. He knew that he'd done the right thing by sending her home but it didn't help very much. He wanted to be with her both in and out of work and it made him see how difficult life was going to be in the coming months when he felt like this. Maybe the best solution would be to hand in his notice, only he hated the thought of letting everyone down. Niall had told him that he'd had problems finding anyone suitable to join the team, and it didn't seem fair to create havoc by leaving before his contract ended. Talk about finding himself between the devil and the deep blue sea!

Jessica's husband, Simon, had arrived by the time Nick got back to the maternity unit so Nick took him into the office and explained what had happened. The poor man was obviously upset about missing the birth of his daughter but Nick assured him that he wouldn't have been able to stay with his wife during the operation and that seemed to cheer him up. Nick took him to the ward then went to see if Niall had come back from his meeting yet. He was in his office so Nick tapped on the door and went in.

'How did it go?'

'More or less how you'd imagine.' Niall sighed wearily. 'The only thing the board of trustees seems to care about is that the hospital shouldn't be involved in any litigation. They kept banging on about how much it could cost the trust if Jodie Carmichael's father *and* Hutchins decide to sue. They don't seem to give a damn about the fact that this department's reputation is on the line.'

'Money is usually the driving force behind most decisions,' Nick observed flatly. He shrugged when Niall looked at him because he didn't want to have to explain that remark. Money had had a huge bearing on the events surrounding his brother's accident but he wasn't there to talk about his experiences. 'Everything is brought down to columns of figures nowadays and people don't seem to matter all that much.'

'That's very true, but it's not the way we operate here,' Niall said firmly, standing up. 'Maintaining the reputation of this department is vital and the last thing we want is our patients thinking that they can't trust us. Hutchins has caused a lot of damage by what he's done and there's bound to be repercussions, which is why I don't want anything else to go wrong. We need to ensure that this department is running perfectly from now on.'

'I'm sure the staff will agree with you about that,' Nick concurred. 'From what I've seen so far, everyone who works here is highly motivated.'

'It's a good team,' Niall agreed, walking to the filing cabinet and opening the top drawer. 'Our biggest problem at the moment is that we're carrying a couple of vacancies. I've told Martin Hopkins that I want them advertised, a.s.a.p.'

'Which posts still need filling?' Nick asked, frowning.

'We need another junior reg, preferably one with a bit of experience rather than an absolute beginner, plus an experienced midwife.' Niall took a file out of the drawer. 'I'm hoping to tempt back some of the staff who used to work here and maybe offer the midwife's post as a job share... Now, there's a thought! I wonder if Sarah would fancy it?'

'Sarah?' Nick queried.

'My wife.' Niall laughed. 'She was a midwife on this very unit until she left to have our son, Jack. That's how we met, in fact, when I came to work here. Like you, I'd been working overseas for long periods of time and I was determined to get the department running exactly how I wanted it to. Sarah soon set me straight! She made me see that I needed to be less rigid in my thinking and it's mainly thanks to her that the department has earned such a good reputation, in fact. Anyway, Jack started school last September so it could be the perfect time for Sarah to come back to work on a part-time basis.'

'Sounds like a good idea,' Nick agreed, trying not to let his feelings show. They exchanged a few more pleasantries before Nick left. He still needed to speak to Margaret Carmichael so he went straight back to the maternity unit. However, as he made his way up the stairs, he couldn't hold his feelings at bay any longer. Maybe it was crazy, but he'd actually felt *envious* when he'd heard Niall speaking so lovingly about his wife just now. He would have given ten years of his life to be able to enjoy that kind of closeness with Katie but it would never happen…

Could it?

His heart began to pound because it was the first time he'd allowed himself to wonder if he could have a normal life. He was almost afraid to test out the idea in case the usual feelings came roaring back, but it didn't happen. Maybe it wasn't a complete impossibility after all. It all depended how Katie would feel when he told her about Mike's accident. Would she understand? Or would she believe that he was to blame in some way?

He had no idea but it was scary to wonder about it when it seemed that his whole future could be hanging in the balance.

CHAPTER NINE

THE next few days flew past and, thankfully, there were no more unpleasant surprises. Evidently, the newspapers had found something else to write about because there were only a couple of reporters still hanging about outside the hospital.

Katie was relieved that everything had quietened down, although there was no denying that the press coverage had caused a lot of unrest. Niall took the unprecedented step of writing to every patient on their books to assure them that their privacy was of the upmost importance. Katie hoped it would work but she wasn't surprised when a couple of people phoned to say that they'd decided to attend Hunter's Green Hospital in future for their antenatal care.

The only good thing to come out of it all was that Margaret Carmichael had told her daughter what had been going on and the girl had taken the news far better than anyone had imagined she would. It seemed that Jodie was determined to prove how well she could cope with looking after her baby and had told the police and Social Services that she would like to take him home when she was discharged. The little boy had been moved from the special baby care unit and was currently in the nursery, and Jodie was spending a lot of time with him. She'd decided to call him Ben and all the staff agreed that she would cope very well with the demands of a new baby so long as she had support from her family.

Katie was determined to get everything back onto as even a keel as possible after all the upset so she called a staff meeting on the morning of New Year's Eve. Julie Davies, their junior registrar, was back at work that day after her bout of flu, and Rosie had phoned to say that she would be coming in to work the late shift. Life was slowly getting back to normal and Katie was anxious to impress on everyone that they must put the unpleasantness behind them and look forward to the new year.

'I know it's been a very difficult time for the department but we need to put it all behind us,' she began once everyone had gathered in the staffroom. 'The press seem to have grown tired of hounding us so let's hope they'll latch onto some other story and leave us alone.'

'Do we know how they got hold of all that information in the first place?' Abbey piped up.

Katie sighed. 'We have a pretty good idea who was responsible, but I can't tell you the person's name because he's threatened to take legal action if he's cited. All I can say is that it isn't anyone attached to this department.'

'That's awful,' Alison Webster, one of the community midwives, exclaimed. 'You mean to say that the culprit is going to get off scot-free after all the damage he's caused?'

'It looks like it.' Katie glanced round when the door opened, feeling her heart perform a small hiccup of delight when Nick came into the room. She'd seen very little of him since the day he'd taken Jessica Morris to Theatre. He'd been doing a lot of work in the clinic and she'd been busy in the unit so that their paths had crossed only a couple of times in the past few days. Now she found herself drinking in every detail and had to force herself to stop because it was stupid to carry on this way when Nick had made it clear that he wasn't interested in her.

The thought brought a sudden lump to her throat and she had to swallow hard before she could continue. 'The trustees are anxious to avoid litigation so they intend to let the matter drop. Maybe it's for the best, too, because the hospital could do without any more bad publicity at the moment. Though we may yet have Derek Carmichael to deal with if he decides to sue.'

'One of my mums was very concerned about it all when I saw her yesterday,' Alison told her. 'Her husband works for the Ministry of Defence and she's afraid that information about where they live might leak out. Apparently, he has a highly sensitive job and they're worried about any possible repercussions. She told me that she's not sure if she still wants to have her baby at Dalverston General.'

'She isn't the only one, I'm afraid,' Katie confirmed sadly. 'I've had two mums ring up to say that they intend to transfer to Hunter's Green for their antenatal care.'

'Make that four,' Nick put in, drawing all eyes to him. He shrugged, but Katie could tell he was upset about what had happened. 'We had two mums cancel their appointments this morning for the same reason. I've just spoken to the consultant at Hunter's Green and he told me that they've had about a dozen enquiries in the past few days, asking how to go about registering with them. If it carries on like this we'll have nobody left.'

'It's even worse than I thought,' Katie said worriedly. 'And there's nothing we can do to stop what's happening either. We can't put out a press release to explain that it wasn't our fault because of the risk of legal action being taken against us.'

'The board of trustees wouldn't countenance it,' Nick confirmed. 'I've just been to see Niall and told him what had happened. He got straight on to Martin Hopkins but Hopkins refused point blank to do anything about it even though the reputation of this whole department is at stake.'

'It isn't fair!' Abbey declared. 'We all work so hard and then something like this happens and ruins everything.'

'It's not going to do much for us personally either,' Julie put in anxiously. 'I was hoping to get a really good reference when I leave at the end of my rotation, but it's not going to be worth very much after all the bad publicity we've had. I was talking to a friend who works in the obs and gynae unit at St Jude's in London and she told me that everyone there is talking about what's been happening in Dalverston. The consensus is that the department isn't being run properly and the most worrying thing of all is that anyone who works here might have problems getting another job.'

'It's even worse than I thought!' Katie exclaimed. 'I was hoping it would blow over eventually, but it sounds as though it's going to cause ripples for a long time to come.'

'The last thing we need to do is to start panicking,' Nick said firmly. 'OK, so we've had some bad press recently but we have to carry on and not let it get us down. We know how hard we work and how high the standards are here so let's focus on that. Forget all the rest and just concentrate on doing our jobs is the best advice I can think of.'

Katie hoped he was right but she could tell how uneasy everyone was feeling. She couldn't blame them because nobody wanted to be associated with a hospital which offered a poor standard of care. The meeting broke up a short time later and she sighed when she realised that Nick had stayed behind to speak to her.

'Thanks for trying to rally the troops. It's upsetting for them to hear that staff from other hospitals believe we're to blame for what's gone on recently.'

'It's a crying shame,' he said bluntly. 'The standards of care here are second to none. Niall is furious about what's happened and I can't blame him.'

'He's worked really hard since he took over as head of department. Granted, standards were high even before then but there's no doubt that he's made a huge difference. He's made it a policy only to hire staff with the very highest qualifications, which is no mean feat because most experienced staff want to work in London or Manchester or some other big city.'

'It was the high standards that made me decide to apply for this post.'

Nick came over and perched on the edge of the desk. Katie bit her lip because he was so close to her now that she could smell the fresh, soapy scent of his skin. Her hands clenched when another waft of the aroma assailed her as he leant forward to pick up a pen. It was sheer torture to be so close to him and not be able to touch him but she remembered what had happened the last time only too clearly.

'Oh, I see.' Her voice sounded thready from the effort of maintaining her control and she hurried on. 'So are you worried in case working here will have a detrimental effect on your career?'

'No. I'm not planning on going any higher up the ladder so it won't make any difference to me.'

'What do you mean?' she asked in surprise. 'Surely you want a consultant's post eventually, don't you?'

'Not really. My main aim has always been to learn as much as I can for the benefit of my patients. That's why I've moved about—so I could gain valuable experience. I'm not really interested in professional glory, to be perfectly honest.'

'But it isn't just a case of covering yourself in glory! The higher up the ladder you go, the more freedom you have to do things the way *you* want them to be done.'

'I'm afraid I don't see it like that,' he stated, and she was struck by the determination in his voice. Obviously, Nick had made up his mind about this and she guessed that he wouldn't easily change it. 'The higher you climb the less time you have to spend doing the job you're trained to do. Niall spends much of his time in meetings and I'm not interested in that side of things. I want to help people, not spend my days balancing budgets.'

'Well, I think that's a wonderful attitude, Nick,' she told him sincerely. 'So many people go into medicine nowadays because they see it as a good career move, but not you, obviously. You're not motivated by a desire for money and power but by the need to help people and I think that's a fantastic attitude to have in such a materialistic world.'

'Don't try putting me on a pedestal, Katie,' he said roughly. 'I don't deserve it. I'm only doing what I have to do.'

'What do you mean by "have to do"? I don't understand, Nick.'

'That I made my choices about how I'd live my life some years ago, but I'm no saint, I assure you.'

'And those choices you made—did they have anything to do with your brother?' she said, watching him closely so that she saw the pain that flashed into his eyes.

'Yes.' He abruptly stood up and she jumped when he tossed the pen onto the desk. 'Anyway, this isn't doing much to restore the good name of the department so I'd better get some work done.' He went to the door then paused and glanced back. 'I forgot to ask if you were going to the New Year's Eve ball tonight.'

'Probably,' she murmured, because she was still trying to assimilate what she'd learned. Nick's career choices had been influenced by his brother's death and she couldn't deny that she was curious to know what had happened to cause him to make such life-changing decisions on the strength of it.

'I'll see you there, then, I expect.'

'Do I take it that you're going with Mel?' she asked, hoping he couldn't tell how painful she found the idea.

'Yes. I'm looking forward to it, too. It should be fun.'

Nick gave her a quick smile then left. Katie followed him out of the room but there was a hollow feeling in the pit of her stomach all of a sudden. Had Nick made a point of telling her that he was looking forward to spending the evening with Mel because he was worried that he might have revealed too much about himself? Was it his way of making sure she understood that it hadn't meant anything?

It seemed to add up and she couldn't pretend that it didn't hurt to know how little he cared for her when she cared so much about him.

Nick had arranged to meet Mel in the foyer at seven o'clock that night. The ball was being held at a hotel in the centre of the town and minibuses had been laid on to ferry the staff to and from the venue. He showered and changed as soon as he got back to his room but, despite his earlier assertions to the contrary, he wasn't looking forward to the evening. Spending the evening with Mel when he wanted to spend it with Katie was going to be a test of his resolve.

He sighed heavily because he'd seen the hurt on Katie's face when he'd told her how much he was looking forward to the evening, but what else could he have done? He'd needed to batten down his own emotions because hearing her praise him for his dedication had been too difficult to deal with. He'd felt like such a fraud that all he'd wanted to do was set the record straight, only it wouldn't have been right to do it then. If—and it was still a very big *if* at this stage—he told her the full story about his brother's accident he wanted to choose the right moment to do it. He certainly hadn't wanted to spill it all out in the office when they could have been interrupted so he'd taken the only route open to him, but it didn't make him feel good to know that he'd upset her.

He groaned because his life was becoming increasingly fraught of late and that wasn't what he'd planned. His time at Dalverston had been meant to be a period of recuperation and learning but he'd never factored Katie into the equation, had he? She made him feel things he'd never felt before, want things he'd never even dreamed of having, and it scared him to think how easily it could all go wrong. What it boiled down to was did he have the courage to tell her the truth when she, too, might think he'd been at fault?

It was a sobering thought and Nick found it difficult to put it out of his mind as he made his way back to the hospital. There was quite a large crowd gathered in the foyer but he couldn't see any sign of Mel. The first of the minibuses arrived so he hung back while some staff from the orthopaedic department piled on board. A couple more buses arrived and once again they were quickly filled. Nick checked his watch, wondering if he'd made a mistake about the arrangements. Maybe Mel had decided to go straight to the hotel and expected him to meet her there. He'd just decided to go and see if she was in her room when one of the other nurses from Paediatrics came hurrying over to him.

'Mel said to tell you that she's very sorry but she won't be able to go tonight, after all. She thinks she's coming down with that rotten flu bug and feels dreadful.' The nurse smiled sympathetically. 'It's such a shame because she was really looking forward to it, too.'

'What a pity. Anyway, thanks for letting me know,' Nick told her, trying to hide his relief as he turned towards the exit. Although he certainly didn't want Mel to be ill, he couldn't deny that it was a big weight off his mind not to have to go to the ball with her.

'Where do you think you're going?' The nurse grasped his arm and briskly steered him towards the very last minibus. 'Mel gave me strict instructions that you were still to go to the ball so come along now.'

'Oh, no, really. There's no need,' Nick protested, but the woman shook her head.

'Sorry, but you aren't getting away *that* easily. Apart from the fact that a spare male is always welcome at these dos, Mel would never forgive me. She was more worried about spoiling *your* evening than missing the dance herself!'

Before Nick could protest any more, he found himself being hustled onto the bus. They were the last to board and the rest of the passengers sent up a loud cheer when they appeared. He quickly sat down on the seat, knowing that he couldn't delay the party any more by causing a fuss. He would just have to go along to the hotel then make his escape whenever he could.

It took just over ten minutes to get into town. Everyone was in very high spirits by the time the bus stopped outside the hotel and Nick found himself swept along with the crowd. He handed over his ticket at the door of the ballroom and went in. He'd been told that the New Year's Eve ball was the highlight of the hospital's social calendar and the room was certainly packed. He spotted Niall by the bar and went to join him when the older man called him over. Niall introduced him to his wife, Sarah, and they exchanged the usual pleasantries, then Abbey appeared and demanded that he dance with her.

Nick couldn't think of an excuse that wouldn't cause offence so followed her onto the dance floor. It was too packed to do much more than shuffle on the spot, but Abbey seemed to enjoy it even if he could hardly wait for the record to end. However, as soon as it finished, the DJ put another one on the deck so he was forced to have a second dance with Abbey because he could hardly abandon her in the middle of the floor. It was a relief when the music stopped and Abbey declared that she was too hot to dance any more.

Nick led her off the floor, hoping to make his excuses and leave, but once again he was thwarted when Abbey tucked her hand through his arm and dragged him over to where the staff from the maternity unit were sitting. Nick said hello to everyone but his mouth seemed to be working independently of his brain. His brain was far too busy taking note of how gorgeous Katie looked. She'd left her light brown hair loose that night and the silky-soft curls bounced around her shoulders each time she moved her head. Nick was no expert when it came to make-up but she'd done something to her eyes and they looked wonderful—huge and luminous. However, it was when she stood up to dance with Pete Gilchrist, and he got a glimpse of her dress, that the real damage was done.

Nick managed to swallow his moan of delight as his eyes feasted on the curves so beautifully displayed by the burgundy dress, but it was a waste of time pretending that he wasn't affected by what he was seeing. How could he pretend that his blood wasn't racing and his heart wasn't pounding when he could *feel* what was happening?

Katie looked so beautiful that he wanted to go straight over to Pete and demand that he take his hands off her, but he could imagine the uproar that would cause. Instead, he had to sit there and behave as though nothing untoward was happening, and it was the hardest thing he'd ever had to do, harder even than coping with the aftermath of Mike's accident. He loved Katie so much and he didn't want any other man to hold her in his arms!

Nick felt the blood drain from his head and knew that it was a good job that he was sitting down because he would have keeled over if he hadn't been. He loved Katie and there was no point lying to himself. He had no idea how it could have happened so quickly but it was true. No wonder he'd been so keyed up of late, so worried about what he should and shouldn't tell her. He'd done the one thing he'd sworn he would never do and now he didn't know how to handle the situation. He was still trying to decide, in fact, when the music ended and Katie came back to the table.

Nick stood up so she could get past him and felt his heart squeeze out a couple of extra beats when her arm brushed his chest. He must have made some sort of sound because she suddenly looked up and it was like being struck by lightning when their eyes met. He wasn't even aware of moving as he took hold of Katie's hand and led her back to the dance floor. Maybe they floated there on air but all of a sudden they were standing in the middle of the throng and it felt the most natural thing in the world to take her in his arms. He drew her towards him and was overcome by pleasure when he realised how perfectly her body fit with his, as though they were two interlocking pieces of the same jigsaw. His eyes misted with sudden tears and he had to blink hard because it felt as though he'd suddenly found a part of him that had been missing.

He drew her even closer, too overcome by the wonder of it all to speak. He couldn't hear the music playing now because of the pounding of his heart but it didn't really matter. They were dancing to their own beat, their own rhythm, and that was more important than anything else. They circled the floor a couple of times before the music ended but Nick couldn't bear to let her go and stood there with his arms around her while he waited for another track to begin. Katie didn't say a word the whole while and her silence was the sweetest thing he'd ever heard because it just seemed to prove how in tune they were with each other.

The DJ put another record on the deck, a slow number this time that brought more couples onto the floor, but he and Katie had their own little space and nobody invaded it. Nick let his hands rest lightly on the back of her waist as they danced together—one step, two— and suddenly each step was pure torture when every time they moved he could feel her body pressing so invitingly against his. Heat flooded through him because there was no way he could hide what was happening to him and he wasn't sure how Katie would feel about his obvious desire for her... And then he felt the hard points of her nipples pressing against his chest and realised that she was every bit as aroused as he was.

'If I don't get you somewhere private soon then I'm going to pass out!' he gritted out from between tightly clenched teeth.

'And we wouldn't want that to happen, would we?' She smiled up at him, her grey eyes shimmering with laughter and passion so that Nick groaned out loud in despair.

'Don't look at me like that! Can't you tell that I'm a man *in extremis*?'

'Then we'd better do something about it, hadn't we?' She took his hand and led him through the crowd. Nick saw several people glance at them but he didn't care what anyone thought. He loved Katie and wanted to be with her and *that* was all that mattered.

They hurried across the hotel's lobby, stopping only long enough to collect Katie's coat before leaving the hotel. As luck would have it there was a taxi pulling up outside so Nick opened the door and Katie got in while he told the driver where to take them. The drive back to the hospital was even quicker than the journey there but to Nick it felt as though a whole year had passed by the time they drew up in front of the hospital. He paid the driver then, hand in hand, they walked back to the staff wing where he let them in. He stopped and turned Katie to face him, wanting her to be completely sure about what they were doing. 'If this isn't what you want, Katie, then just say so.'

'But it is. I don't have any doubts, Nick, but how about you? Are you sure this is the right thing for you?'

'Yes. I'm sure. I want this, Katie. I want it more than I've wanted anything ever before,' he admitted with soul-searing honesty.

'Good.'

She smiled as she reached up and kissed him gently on the mouth and it felt as though every scrap of emotion he'd held in check suddenly exploded from him. When she led him to the stairs, he didn't hesitate and certainly didn't have any more second thoughts because it was what they both wanted. Katie wanted him as much as he wanted her and it felt as though he'd been offered a glimpse of heaven to know it.

They went straight to her room because it was nearest. Katie unlocked the door then held out her hand. Nick took it, feeling the tremor that ran through her as she led him inside and switched on the lamp. He turned her around and kissed her, glorying in the way she immediately responded as soon as his mouth touched hers. The kiss ran on and on, as though they were both so hungry for the taste of each other that they couldn't bear it to end. Then, slowly, he drew back, holding her gaze as he unbuttoned her coat and slid it off her shoulders.

'You look really beautiful tonight, Katie.'

'Thank you. So do you.' She smiled as she reached up and unfastened his tie. She slid it out from under his collar and dropped it on the floor beside the bed then looked at him. 'You next.'

'Turn and turn about, eh?' Nick chuckled as he turned her round and deftly slid the zipper down the back of her dress. He peeled the two edges apart then had to stop for a moment while he allowed himself the delight of scattering kisses down the length of her spine, and felt the shudder of pleasure that ran through her.

She turned to face him again, her eyes cloudy with passion as she helped him out of his jacket then it was his turn again so he dispensed with her dress. All she had on now was her underwear and his blood pressure rocketed up another couple of degrees as he took stock of the creamy mounds of her breasts beneath the black lace bra, and the matching triangle of lace at her hips.

'I thought you looked beautiful wearing that dress but you look even more lovely without it,' he forced out because his breathing was causing him no end of problems all of a sudden.

'Thank you—again,' she whispered, her voice sounding thready and strained as she began unbuttoning his shirt. She managed to work one button free, then two, but her hands were shaking so hard now that the next one defeated her. Nick solved the problem by dragging the shirt over his head and tossing it aside but the look on her face as she studied his bare chest made him wonder if he'd been a little too hasty.

'Katie, I…'

'You're so beautiful, Nick.' Her hands fluttered against his chest for a moment before she laid them flat against his skin and he could hear the awe and wonderment in her voice. 'I never realised before that a man's body could be so beautiful.'

Nick closed his eyes, hoping it would help him keep control if he didn't look at her. That confession had touched him so deeply that he felt raw, as though every nerve ending was suddenly exposed and aching. When her hands began gently caressing his skin, he gasped aloud because it wasn't like anything he'd ever experienced before. When he'd made love with a woman in the past it had been out of physical need and this was so different that he couldn't begin to compare the two. This time his emotions as well as his senses were engaged and the thought finally tipped him over the edge.

He swept her into his arms and kissed her, hearing the soft murmur she made and knowing instinctively that it was pleasure that had prompted it. Katie wanted him every bit as much as he wanted her and the proof of that was the way she clung to him and kissed him back, her mouth opening so that his tongue could slide into her mouth. His body was pulsing with desire now but he wasn't ashamed of letting her feel how much he needed her. He certainly didn't want to hide his feelings because he wanted Katie to know how much this meant to him. When he lifted her into his arms and carried her to the bed there wasn't a doubt in his mind that they were doing the right thing.

He laid her down then bent and kissed her: her mouth, her nose, her eyelids; anywhere and everywhere he could place a kiss he did. Then he unclipped her bra and kissed her breasts, drawing her nipples into his mouth and suckling her until she moaned out her need, but there were still more pleasures to come for them both.

Nick knelt beside the bed and slowly pulled off the tiny scrap of lace that covered her hips then kissed her there, gentle kisses that soon made the passion burning inside them build to unbearable proportions. Katie was just as desperate as he was when he shed the rest of his clothes and lay down beside her, just as eager to feel him inside her as he was to be there.

He kissed her on the mouth as he entered her, trying to be gentle so he wouldn't hurt her, but their desire was simply too fierce to hold back. They made love with a fervour that verged on desperation and when it was over and Katie was lying in his arms, her body relaxed and at ease, Nick knew that he'd just touched heaven. Maybe he didn't deserve such happiness but nothing—*nothing*—could ever take away the beauty of this night from him!

CHAPTER TEN

GREY winter light was filtering into the room when Katie awoke. Just for a second she couldn't understand why she felt so happy before everything came rushing back and she felt her heart swell with tenderness when she turned and saw Nick lying beside her. There wasn't much room in the narrow single bed so knowing that he'd opted for the discomfort of staying with her instead of going back to his own room filled her with happiness all of a sudden. She leant over and kissed him, laughing when his arms immediately went around her as he gathered her close.

'I thought you were asleep!'

'That was what I wanted you to think.' His smile was smug. 'I knew you wouldn't be able to resist taking advantage of me.'

'Oh, did you, now?' She pretended to glare at him. 'Very sure of yourself, aren't you, Dr Lawson? Do I take it that most women find you irresistible?'

'But of course! They're just putty in my hands.' He flexed his fingers and leered at her. Katie laughed.

'Hmm, I'll take your word for it.'

'You mean that you don't feel the same?' He drew her closer and smiled into her eyes in a way that made her insides begin to melt. 'I must be slipping. Maybe I'd better have another go at convincing you about my prowess as a lover...'

Katie sighed when his lips found hers. She most certainly wasn't going to tell him that she didn't need convincing! She twined her arms around his neck and gave herself up to the sheer pleasure of making love with the man of her dreams. Maybe Nick didn't feel as strongly about her as she did about him, but he must feel something, surely? It was scary suddenly to be beset by doubts so she chased them from her head because she didn't want anything to spoil this moment, and it was every bit as wonderful as she could have wished. Nick cradled her in his arms afterwards as they slowly came back to earth.

'You blow my mind, Katie Denning.' He buzzed her cheek with his lips then sighed. 'I never understood that saying about not being able to think straight but now I know exactly what it means. It feels as though all my thoughts are floating about inside my head and I can't seem to drag them together and put them back into order.'

'So you haven't felt this way with anyone else?' she asked quietly, wanting to settle her fears once and for all. Would Nick tell her that he cared for her if she prompted him? She hoped so because then she could tell him how she felt, but she was afraid to rush things.

'No. Oh, I'm not trying to claim that I've lived the life of a monk because it wouldn't be true. But I can honestly say that I've never felt this way about anyone before,' he admitted, dropping another kiss onto her nose.

'That's good to hear,' she said, smiling at him. 'So what's made the difference this time?'

'You.'

He pulled her into his arms and kissed her again, and Katie knew that she had to be content with that even though it wasn't as much as she'd hoped for. Maybe Nick needed a bit more time to come to terms with his feelings so she mustn't try and question him again. She had a feeling that his reticence was all tied up with what had happened in the past so she would have to be patient and let him tell her in his own good time how he felt.

They were both off duty that day so when Nick suggested that they make the most of their time off and drive out to the country, she eagerly agreed. They had a quick breakfast then set off, taking the road that wound its way across Dalverston moor. There was very little traffic about so they parked the car at the side of the road and followed the footpath to Dalverston Falls, a local beauty spot. Even though it was freezing cold, the view from the top of the waterfall was spectacular and they stayed there until their feet felt as though they were in danger of freezing to the rocks then went back to the car and found a country pub that served meals.

'This is delicious,' Katie declared, forking up a hearty mouthful of steaming hot lasagne.

'Good. It might make up for missing the buffet last night,' Nick said, grinning at her. Like her, he was wearing jeans and a heavy sweater under his jacket and he looked so gorgeous that Katie couldn't resist leaning across the table and kissing him.

'Mmm, nice. I like the taste of garlic,' he joked, licking his lips. 'It added a definite something to the kiss that had been lacking before.'

'Cheek!' She glared at him. 'I'd advise you to be very careful what you say or you won't get any more kisses.'

'And that would never do, would it?' He lifted her hand off the table and turned it over so he could press his mouth to her palm.

Katie shivered when she felt the tip of his tongue licking her skin. Even though it had been only a few hours since they'd made love, she could feel passion stirring again. When Nick suggested that they go back to the hospital after they'd finished their lunch, she didn't object.

They drove straight back and without uttering a word went to her room. This time their love-making was more gentle and less fevered but it was no less arousing because of that. Katie longed to tell Nick how much she loved him but once again she held back because she sensed he wasn't ready to hear it. She could only hope the time would come when he would be ready but she'd gone into this with her eyes open and she knew there was a chance it might never happen. All she could do was pray that Nick would come to love her as much as she loved him.

Katie was back on duty the next day, working the middle shift from eleven in the morning until eight in the evening. She and Nick had spent the whole of the previous day together in the end. He'd only left her at midnight, in fact, because he'd been due in work at six and had needed to get some sleep. Katie smiled to herself as she made her way to the office for the handover because sleep would have been the last thing on their minds if he'd stayed! Now she was looking forward to seeing him again so much that her heart leapt when she opened the office door and found him in there.

'Nick!' she began happily, then stopped when she saw the grim expression on his face. 'What's wrong now?' she demanded, hurrying towards him.

'A and E just phoned to say that they have Abbey down there. They think she may have been drug-raped.'

'No! Oh, how awful,' Katie exclaimed in horror. 'When did it happen? Do they know?'

'Probably on New Year's Eve but Abbey can't remember what happened. Apparently, she woke up in her
flat yesterday evening and had no recollection of what
had gone on the night before. She phoned her parents
and they drove down from Cumbria and insisted on
bringing her to hospital.'

'Is she badly hurt?'

'I've no idea. I've just spoken to Sean Fitzgerald but
he wouldn't tell me very much.' He shrugged. 'Patient
confidentiality and all that, so I can't really blame him.
Jean's gone to see her so maybe she'll be able to tell
us a bit more when she gets back.'

'Poor Abbey. It's such a terrible thing to happen to
any woman but when it's someone you know...' She
shuddered and Nick put his arms round her and hugged
her.

'I know, sweetheart. It's horrible. She's going to need
a lot of support from her friends to get through this. I'd
really like to get my hands on the scumbag who did
this to her!'

'I wonder who it was.' Katie frowned. 'If it happened
on New Year's Eve, does that mean it was someone
from the hospital? Abbey was at the ball and I don't
imagine that she went anywhere else after it ended.'

'I expect the police will want to question everyone
who was there,' Nick said flatly. 'Every single man
present on the night is a possible suspect.'

'Apart from you,' Katie pointed out. 'You spent the
night with me, remember?'

'How could I forget?' he murmured, his eyes holding
hers in a look that made her heartbeat quicken. All of
a sudden, Katie knew that she had to tell him how she
felt. Maybe it *was* too soon and Nick wasn't ready to
hear it, but she couldn't hold back any longer. She

needed to tell him that she loved him because it was too important not to say the words.

'Nick,' she began, then stopped when the door opened. There was just time for Nick to release her before Jean came bustling into the room. Katie breathed a sigh that was compounded of relief for not having been caught out and impatience at being interrupted. However, she soon forgot about her own concerns when Jean started to tell them about Abbey.

'She's in a really bad way,' the older woman said sadly. 'There's some really nasty bruises on her cheek and shoulders, plus some internal damage—vaginal tearing and bruising, things like that. She asked me to check her notes because she wanted to know how much damage had been done,' Jean added by way of explanation in case they were wondering how she came to know all the intimate details.

'Let's keep that between ourselves,' Katie suggested hurriedly. 'Abbey might not want people knowing what's happened.'

'It's not going to be possible to keep it quiet,' Jean pointed out. 'The police arrived as I was leaving and I imagine they are going to want to interview everyone who was at the ball on New Year's Eve.'

'Can Abbey remember anything at all about what happened?' Nick put in. 'I've read that some victims of drug-rape have flashbacks.'

'She remembers dancing with various people and thinks someone bought her a drink but she can't remember who it was.' Jean shrugged. 'There were enough people there on the night so someone must have seen who she was with.'

'I know this is a horrible thing to ask but is there any

trace evidence the police could use to identify him—
semen or saliva?' Katie asked with a shudder.

'I don't know. She's had the usual tests done—blood
and a hair sample to try and identify the drug she was
given, but they're still waiting for the results to come
back from the lab.' Jean grimaced. 'However, I did
overhear one of the A and E staff saying that they were
waiting for the forensic team to arrive so I expect they'll
do the rest.'

Katie nodded, wishing there was something she could
do to help her friend. She couldn't begin to imagine
what Abbey must be going through. Nick had to leave
just then because he was needed in clinic so she and
Jean did the handover. There was just one mum in the
delivery suites and she'd opted for a water birth so Katie
went to check on her as soon as the formalities were
completed. Trish Johnson, one of their part-timers who
worked three mornings a week, was with the patient and
it was obvious that she was eager for news about
Abbey.

Katie wanted to clamp down on any gossip for
Abbey's sake so she told Trish firmly that she had no
idea what was happening. It seemed to do the trick and
left them free to concentrate on the delivery. It was
Suzanne Whalley's second child and she'd prepared for
the birth by working out a birth plan. Katie knew that
Suzanne had been disappointed when she'd had her first
child at a hospital in Essex because she'd felt the whole
process had been too mechanical. She was determined
that this baby would be born with as little intervention
as possible and had set out guidelines about what she
wanted. They would stick to the plan so long as there
weren't any complications.

Katie got the room ready while Trish finished helping

Suzanne to undress. The birthing pool had been filled with warm water and was all ready so she dimmed the lights then put the tape Suzanne had selected in the player. Some mums enjoyed listening to music while they gave birth and others preferred total silence. Suzanne's husband came in with a bag of scented candles so they placed them around the room and then Suzanne arrived.

Katie helped her into the pool. Suzanne was fully dilated and her contractions were coming at regular intervals so she guessed it wouldn't take long for the baby to arrive. Suzanne didn't want gas and air or any drugs so it was just a case of monitoring her progress and making sure the baby didn't become distressed. Most mums who opted for water births had very positive attitudes and Katie had found that this helped enormously. She wasn't surprised when an hour later Suzanne's baby made its appearance. It was a little boy, which was what both mother and father had been hoping for, so it was a very special moment for all of them.

Katie took the baby and carried him over to the table so she could check him over. He was alert yet calm as so many babies were when they were born in water. Trish had delivered the afterbirth by the time Katie took the child back and handed him to his father, so that was another thing accomplished without any fuss. Suzanne hadn't suffered any tearing either, so she could be moved straight to a ward. However, Katie decided to give the parents some time alone together with their child and left them in the delivery suite with instructions to ring the bell if they needed anything.

Nick was just passing the door when she left the room and he stopped when he saw her. 'How did it go?'

'Perfect. When I have a child I'm definitely going to

opt for a water birth. It's much less stressful for both the mother and the baby, isn't it?'

'It seems to be.'

Katie frowned when she heard the rather terse note in his voice all of a sudden. 'Is something wrong?'

'No, of course not.' He glanced at his watch. 'I'll have to run. I only popped back to fetch some notes that had gone missing from one of the files. If I don't get back to the clinic soon we'll have a riot on our hands and that would never do, would it?'

'No, it wouldn't,' Katie agreed, chuckling at the thought of all the pregnant mums rioting around the clinic. 'Maybe we can have a cup of coffee together later on. I'm due for a break at two if that fits in with you.'

Nick shook his head. 'No can do, I'm afraid. I'm going to be tied up in clinic all day. There's a couple of mums who need repeat scans so Niall has asked me to be on hand in case of any problems.'

'Not to worry.' Katie shrugged, trying to be philosophical about his refusal. After all, the patients had to come first. 'I'll catch up with you at some point, I expect.'

'Of course.'

Nick treated her to a quick smile then hurried away. Katie went back to check on Suzanne and her baby, determined not to read anything into the fact that Nick hadn't made any definite arrangements to see her again that day. He'd been too busy to worry about it, she told herself, so there was no point getting paranoid.

Her heart suddenly lifted because she couldn't imagine Nick *not* wanting to be with her after the last couple of days!

*   *   *

Nick was glad when it was time to go off duty. It had been a stressful day for many reasons but most stressful of all was that comment Katie had made about how she intended to have her children. It seemed to have cut right through to the very heart of his being and he'd found it difficult to deal with the shock waves it had caused.

He went back to his room and sat on the bed while he thought about it, and about everything else that had happened in the past few days. He'd never intended to get involved with Katie but it had happened and he couldn't pretend that his life hadn't been turned on its head because of it. He'd sworn that he would devote himself to work in memory of his brother, but now he could no longer picture himself living that lonely existence. Work might have been enough in the past but now he wanted more: Katie and those children she'd spoken about; a home and everything that other people took for granted. But did he *deserve* any of those things? Was it *right* for him to seek personal happiness?

He couldn't put his hand on his heart and answer yes to either of those questions and that was the most scary part of it all. He had to be sure about what he was doing because it wasn't just his life that would be affected by any decisions he made. Katie's life would be equally affected and he wouldn't be able to live with himself if he did anything to cause her pain.

He took a deep breath but there was no hiding from the truth. It would be better to end this now rather than run the risk of ruining her life.

Katie managed to slip down to the assessment ward during her evening break. She'd phoned A and E and one of the staff had told her that Abbey had been moved there while they waited for the test results to come back from the lab. Katie popped into the shop in the foyer and bought some magazines then went straight to the ward. Abbey was in a bed in the far corner, looking pale and dazed and so unlike the happy, smiling girl Katie had seen two days earlier that she felt a lump come to her throat.

'How are you?' she asked gently, putting the magazines on top of the locker and pulling over a chair.

'I don't know how I feel,' Abbey whispered, her eyes brimming with tears. 'Why did it happen to me, Katie? I mean, did I do something wrong, something to *make* it happen?'

'Of course you didn't,' Katie said firmly, taking her hand. 'No woman makes a thing like this happen to her so don't you dare blame yourself.'

'That's what the police doctor said when he came to collect the forensic evidence.' Abbey managed a wobbly smile. 'He was really kind and told me that he'd get all the tests done as quickly as possible.'

'Did he seem to think he'd found anything useful?' Katie asked, careful how to phrase the question, but Abbey still shuddered.

'Not really. Whoever did it used a condom. It's good in one way because there's less risk of me having caught an STD or anything worse, but not so good in another way because the police might not be able to trace who attacked me.'

'And you can't remember who you were with before it happened?' Katie prompted.

'No. My mum keeps asking me that but it's all so vague. When I woke up I felt as though I had a massive hangover but I knew it couldn't be that because I don't drink very much. I kept coming to and passing out again so it wasn't until late last night that I realised something had happened to me…' She stopped and frowned. 'I remember someone asking me if I wanted a drink but I'm not sure who it was.'

'Let's hope someone else remembers who you were with,' Katie said quickly, not wanting to upset her any more. 'Somebody is bound to have seen who you were talking to.'

'The police said they're going to interview everyone who was at the ball that night.' Abbey bit her lip. 'That means everybody's going to know what's happened.'

'I'm sure they'll be discreet,' Katie assured her, although there was little hope of keeping a lid on it once the police started asking questions.

She stayed another few minutes then left when Abbey's parents came back. They were going to take her home with them as soon as she was discharged so Katie told her that she thought it was a good idea not to be on her own. She went back to the maternity unit and helped hand round the bedtime drinks then got everyone settled for the night. A couple of mums were doing last-minute feeds in the nursery so she spent a few minutes chatting to them. Then the bell rang. Katie went to the door and was surprised when she found Larry Price, the anaesthetist, outside. He had his wife with him and she was obviously in a lot of pain so Katie found a wheelchair and whisked her straight to the examination room.

'Becks only realised she was pregnant on New Year's Day,' Larry told her anxiously. 'She was going to make an appointment with our GP in the morning. We were just getting ready to go out tonight when she started having pains and realised she was bleeding. A and E are dealing with a bad traffic accident so I brought her straight to you. If it's a miscarriage you're the best people to deal with it.'

'I'll get Julie to take a look at her,' Katie assured him, hurrying to the phone. Once she was sure the young registrar was being paged, she went back to the bed. She knew Becks quite well because Becks had worked in Theatre before she'd taken a job with a local nursing agency.

'Can't stay away from the place, can you?' she said, helping Becks out of her coat.

'It's like home from home,' Becks replied, bravely trying to smile.

They got her undressed and onto the bed but Julie still hadn't arrived so Katie went back to the phone and asked the switchboard to page her again because it was urgent. Julie phoned her back almost immediately to say that she was in A and E, dealing with a patient who'd been involved in an RTA and was eight months pregnant. The young registrar didn't know how long she would be there and Katie knew they couldn't wait for her to get back. She would have to contact the next doctor rostered on call that night and it just happened to be Nick.

She had him paged then got everything ready so they wouldn't waste any more time when he got there. She was just moving the ultrasound scanner over to the bed when he arrived and her heart filled with joy. She smiled at him, wondering if he could tell how much she loved him from the expression on her face. It was impossible to hide her feelings but if he did notice he didn't give any sign, and a chill rippled through her. Maybe it was silly to get upset but she couldn't help it when she longed to know if he returned her feelings.

'When did you first start having pains?' Nick asked after he'd introduced himself to Becks.

'Late on this afternoon. It was just a niggly little pain at first, a bit like when you get a stitch in your side when you've been hurrying,' she explained. 'I took no notice at first because I was too busy getting dinner ready.'

'Like any devoted wife should do,' Larry interjected, making a brave attempt at levity although Katie could tell how worried he really was.

'Like any woman who's got a useless husband, you mean,' Becks retorted. 'After we'd eaten, I went upstairs to get changed because we were going to the cinema and that's when I realised I was bleeding. Larry made me lie down but the pains started getting worse.'

'I see. Let's take a look at you and see what we can find.' Nick gently examined Becks, pausing when she cried out when he touched her lower abdomen. 'That seems to be very tender so I think I'll do a scan. I'm going to do a trans-vaginal one, if that's OK with you?'

Katie didn't say anything as she got everything ready but she knew what Nick must suspect if he'd opted to do a vaginal scan instead of the more usual abdominal one. She waited while he covered the transducer wand—the part of the machine which emitted high-frequency sound waves—with a condom and lubricant. Larry was holding Becks's hand and there was complete silence in the room when Nick began.

Katie watched over his shoulder as the images began to appear on the screen and her heart sank when she realised that his suspicions had been correct. Becks had an ectopic pregnancy which meant the baby had started to develop outside her womb. The foetus was growing in her left Fallopian tube and it was a life-threatening condition requiring emergency treatment, so she could understand why Nick looked so grave.

'I'm sorry to have to tell you that it's an ectopic pregnancy,' he explained to the couple. 'The embryo has embedded itself in your left Fallopian tube and we're going to have to remove it before the tube ruptures.'

'Is there anything you can do?' Becks whispered. 'For the baby, I mean.'

'No. I'm very sorry but there's absolutely nothing I can do to save it.' Nick squeezed her hand. 'I know how hard this must be for you but our main concern now is to make sure that you're all right.'

'Will you be able to save her Fallopian tube?' Larry put in, looking very pale.

'I'm not sure until I see how badly damaged it is,' Nick replied honestly. 'An ectopic pregnancy can occur if the tube is already damaged so I'll need to take that into account, and even if the tube was perfectly healthy to begin with then there's bound to have been some damage done to it by the embryo developing inside it. I have to warn you that in most cases the tube has to be removed.'

Becks began to cry. 'That means I'll never have a baby of my own now.'

'No, it doesn't,' Nick said firmly. 'Your chances of getting pregnant will be slightly reduced, but there's no reason why you shouldn't conceive again because you'll still have one healthy Fallopian tube.'

'We'll just have to try that bit harder, then, won't we, love?' Larry told her, obviously trying to remain positive for his wife's sake.

Katie sighed because it was sad to see such a lovely couple going through this awful experience. When Nick asked her to assist him, she readily agreed even though it meant that she'd be late finishing again. They took Becks to Theatre and managed to persuade Larry that it wouldn't be a good idea for him to stay. Nick had decided to go for minimally invasive keyhole surgery, and once again Katie was impressed by his skill as he removed the embryo, placenta and damaged tissue then repaired the torn blood vessels. All things considered, the operation went very well although Nick was upset because he'd had to remove the Fallopian tube and said as much when they left Theatre a short time later.

'It was too badly damaged to be saved,' Katie assured him. 'Plus there would have been a higher risk of Becks having another ectopic pregnancy if you'd left the damaged tube *in situ*.'

'I know.' He sighed. 'It's just that I could see how worried Larry looked when I told them I'd have to remove the tube. They're obviously keen to start a family so it must seem like the worst thing that could have happened to them at this point.'

'Maybe it does at the moment but they'll soon come round. Most couples who find themselves in this situation go on to have a family. You know that as well as I do.'

'Yep. I'm just being an old worrywart, aren't I?'

Katie laughed. 'Well, you said it!'

Nick grinned. 'Meaning that you agree?'

'Yes. You worry far too much, Nick. You can't work miracles. You just have to do the best you can, like we all do.'

'And what if I feel that my best isn't enough? What should I do then?'

Katie's heart leapt because she sensed there was more to that question than a simple need for reassurance.

'Then you have to ask yourself why you're always striving to reach an impossible goal.'

'And what if I already know the answer to that question?'

'Then you need to make some changes to your life.' She took a deep breath. 'This all has to do with your brother, hasn't it? What really happened, Nick? Please, will you tell me?'

CHAPTER ELEVEN

'THIS really isn't the right time,' Nick began, wishing that he'd had the sense not to say anything in the first place. He still wasn't sure what he was going to do about him and Katie so it wouldn't be fair to burden her with his problems at this stage.

'Maybe not, but you need to talk about it at some point.' She looked him squarely in the eyes. 'Your brother's death obviously affected you deeply so did you have counselling afterwards? Did you talk to your family and friends about it even?'

'It was all very complicated,' he said, thinking that must be the biggest understatement of all time. 'My parents were too upset to talk about what had happened so we all tried to cope the best way we could.'

'As a doctor you must know that it isn't always possible to deal with events like that by yourself,' she said quietly.

'I thought I had dealt with it until recently,' Nick admitted truthfully, then looked round when the door to Theatre opened and the scrub nurse appeared. They couldn't talk with someone else there so he quickly changed the subject, relieved to have been let off the hook again. He knew Katie was right and that he did need to talk about what had gone on but, first, he needed to be sure that he was doing the right thing.

'I'll go and have a word with Larry,' he told her, striding to the door. 'He must be anxious for news of Becks.'

'Fine. You carry on. I'm off duty now.'

Nick sighed when he heard the hurt in Katie's voice. She obviously thought he was being deliberately evasive but it wasn't that simple. He left Theatre and went to the waiting-room where Larry was in danger of wearing a hole in the carpet from pacing up and down.

'Becks is fine,' Nick assured him as soon as he went in. 'I had to remove her Fallopian tube because it was too badly damaged to save it, but the main thing is that she's OK. She's in Recovery at the moment and you can see her as soon as you like.'

'Thank heavens!' Larry abruptly sat down on a chair as his legs suddenly gave way. 'I never realised before what it's like when you're waiting for news. My mind's been running riot here!'

'Too much knowledge can be a dangerous thing,' Nick said lightly, wanting to lift the mood for his sake as well as his friend's. He hated feeling as though he was being dishonest with Katie when all he wanted to do was protect her.

'Too right. Ignorance is definitely bliss in a case like this.' Larry ran a trembling hand over his face then held out both his hands and stared at them in amazement. 'Just look at me! I'm shaking like a leaf. Good job I wasn't the one operating tonight.'

'You're bound to be upset because you love Becks and want what's best for her,' Nick assured him.

'That's true.' Larry grimaced. 'I used to be such a selfish bastard but all that was knocked out of me when I met Becks. I'd lay down my life for that woman, and she knows it, too, unfortunately.'

Nick laughed although he couldn't deny how envious he felt of Larry because his friend could be open about his feelings, whereas he had to hide his. 'I'm sure she feels exactly the same way about you.'

'Oh, she does—although wild horses wouldn't drag that confession out of her. Becks likes to keep my feet firmly on the ground and never lets me get above myself. Still, it's all part and parcel of being in love and I, for one, wouldn't change a thing.'

Larry slapped him on the shoulder and left, but Nick stayed where he was, thinking about what the other man had said. It must be wonderful to have that kind of relationship, one based on love and mutual support. It was what he could have with Katie so what was stopping him? Guilt and the fear that he didn't deserve that much happiness? But would Mike have wanted him to live this way, or would he have wanted him to get on with his life?

Nick didn't need to think about the answer to that question because he already knew what it was. Mike had loved life and loved people and he'd have been desolate if he'd thought that he'd been responsible in any way, shape or form for hurting someone else. It was all so clear that Nick was amazed that he hadn't realised it before but he'd been so wrapped up in self-recrimination that he'd lost sight of what really mattered. And what really mattered was Katie and the life they could have together.

He left the waiting-room and ran to the stairs, groaning when his pager started buzzing like a demented wasp. He checked the display as he hurried to the nearest phone, frowning when he saw that it was A and E paging him. He phoned them back and was passed straight over to Julie who was in a panic because the woman injured in the RTA was haemorrhaging badly and the young registrar wasn't sure what to do.

Nick assured her that he'd be straight there and hung up. Even though he was desperate to sort things out with Katie, work had to come first. Anyway, a couple more hours wouldn't make a difference when they had the rest of their lives to be together, and it was the most wonderful feeling of all, to know that he had a future to look forward to.

Katie had put herself down for an extra shift to cover Abbey's absence and consequently was feeling rather jaded after the quick turn-about from lates to earlies when she went into work the following day. She'd hoped that Nick would knock on her door after he'd finished work the previous night but there'd been no sign of him and she had to admit that she was a little concerned in case she'd pushed him too hard about his brother. She wanted only what was best for him so she would make sure that he understood that she didn't intend to press him for any more details until he was ready to talk about what had happened. She was just wondering how to get him on his own when she turned the corner and saw all the staff gathered by the desk, poring over a copy of that day's newspaper.

'Don't tell me we're in the news again!' she exclaimed.

'Just wait till you read it.' Rosie frowned. 'I'd never have believed it of him. He seems so nice. It just goes to show that you can't tell what people are really like, doesn't it?'

'Who do you mean?' Katie asked.

'Nick Lawson, of course! Here, read it for yourself.'

Rosie handed her the newspaper and Katie felt the blood drain from her head when she saw the photograph of Nick splashed across the front page. Her hands were shaking so hard that she could barely hold the paper steady while she read the accompanying article which stated that Dr Nicholas Lawson, a specialist registrar working for Dalverston's troubled maternity unit, had been prosecuted ten years previously for drunk driving following an accident in which his younger brother had been killed. There was a lot more on the inside pages about the wisdom of hiring someone like Nick to work at the hospital, but Katie had stopped reading by that point because she couldn't take in anything else. Nick had driven while he'd been over the limit and killed his own brother?

She handed the paper back and went to her office, needing time on her own to think about what she'd read. She didn't want to believe what the paper had printed but it could explain why Nick seemed so haunted by his brother'd death. Had she been mistaken about him? Wasn't he the person she'd thought him to be? After all, she could hardly claim to be a good judge of character after the mistake she'd made over David...

She pulled herself up short because she wasn't going to fall into the trap of condemning Nick on such flimsy evidence. Only when Nick told her it was true was she going to believe it.

Nick had spent the night in Theatre. Amazingly, the baby—a little girl—had still been alive and he'd been able to deliver her by Caesarean section. However, the mother was so badly injured that not even the team of surgeons who'd worked on her had been able to save her. Nick had stayed on to help long after his part had finished and Morgan Gray, the chief of surgery, made a point of thanking him afterwards.

'I appreciate what you did, Dr Lawson. It's a crying

shame we couldn't save the mother but at least your efforts paid off.' Morgan patted him on the back. 'That was a fine bit of surgery and if you ever feel like a change from Obs and Gynae work just give me a call.'

'Thank you.' Nick summoned a smile but he'd have felt better if they'd managed to save the mother as well as the child. Morgan was going to inform the relatives of the sad news so he showered and changed then left Theatre. It was just gone seven and although he wasn't on duty until eleven he didn't feel like going to bed when he was so wired after what had happened during the night. Katie had mentioned that she was working an extra shift and suddenly the thought of seeing her was too tempting to resist. He could do with a large dollop of Katie's TLC at the moment!

He went straight to the maternity unit, hoping that she wouldn't be too busy to stop and have coffee with him. There was the usual air of bustle about the place but Nick couldn't help noticing how everyone stopped talking when he passed. He frowned when Alison Webster cut him dead when he wished her good morning. He was getting the distinct impression that he was *persona non grata* and he had no idea why until he spotted the morning newspaper lying on the desk.

His heart sank when he saw his photograph and the accompanying headline. Someone—probably that reporter who'd been talking to Hutchins—must have dug up the story about his brother, and Nick could imagine what everyone must be thinking now. He knew that he had to find Katie and tell her the truth, but would she believe him? Even people he'd known for *years* had shunned him after the accident so why should Katie accept that he was telling her the truth? Maybe if he'd told her last night she would have believed his version of events, but it would be much more difficult to convince her this morning.

That wasn't the only thing he had to take into account either. Other people were bound to believe what the papers had printed so did he really want to put Katie in the unenviable position of having to defend him to her colleagues? He knew to his cost how true that old saying was about mud sticking so did he want her name being linked with his and run the risk of her becoming a social outcast as well?

Nick's head was whirling as questions bombarded him from all sides. He knew that he needed to think everything through so left the maternity unit and went back to his room. He lay down on the bed, feeling sick and shaken by what had happened. He could end up losing Katie because of this and that was the worst thing of all, far worse than the thought of people gossiping about him, even worse than the thought of Niall asking him to resign because of the unsavoury publicity he'd brought on the department. Tears suddenly burned his eyes because if he lost Katie then he'd have nothing of any value left.

Katie was a bundle of nerves as she waited for Nick to return. Alison had told her that she'd seen him that morning but there'd been no sign of him since. She clung to the thought that he couldn't possibly have done the awful things he'd been accused of, but each hour that passed made it harder to remain steadfast to that thought. When Niall called her into his office in the middle of the morning and told her tersely that Dr Lawson had requested a leave of absence, she could hardly contain her dismay.

'But why on earth has he done that? Doesn't he realise that people will assume now that what the papers are saying is true?'

'I did try to talk him out of it but he'd made up his mind. He told me that he'd decided to go back to London because he wanted to save the hospital any further embarrassment.' Niall sighed. 'Maybe it was the right decision, too, because Martin Hopkins has been on the phone and he's none too happy about what's happened. This story, coming on top of everything else, won't do the hospital's reputation any good.'

'But there's no proof that it's true!' Katie protested.

'No, there isn't. However, I doubt if that paper would have printed it unless they'd checked their facts beforehand.' Niall sounded troubled. 'I'm not saying that I think Nick is guilty but he's the only one who knows what really happened, and if he isn't prepared to talk about it then there isn't a lot we can say in his defence.'

'Well, I certainly won't believe that Nick is guilty until he tells me that himself!'

Niall nodded but she could see the sympathy in his eyes. 'Then I hope for your sake, Katie, that he gets in touch with you soon. In the meantime, I think it would be best if you told the staff that Dr Lawson is taking some time off.'

'If that's what you want. Did Nick say when he'd be back?'

'No. I'm sorry, he didn't.'

Katie bit her lip because she could tell from Niall's tone that he didn't think that Nick would return to Dalverston only he was too kind to tell her that. She went back to the maternity unit and explained to the others that Nick would be taking some time off until it all blew over. Naturally, that started everyone speculating and her heart ached as she listened to them theorising about whether or not Nick had done what the papers had said he had. She desperately wanted to defend him but how could she when she knew no more than they did? That was what hurt most of all, the fact that Nick hadn't even bothered to see her and explain before he'd left. Did she really mean so little to him that he could just cut her out of his life without a second thought?

The following few weeks were a blur. Nick spent his days wandering the streets of London. He had no idea where he'd been when he got back to the poky little bedsit he'd rented close to Euston station. Faces and places all merged into a meaningless nothing because there was just one face he longed to see, one place he wanted to be. He wanted to be in Dalverston with Katie but how could he go back there and ruin her life?

In the end, he decided that he had to do something so phoned the Worlds Together office and told them that he was available if they needed anyone at short notice. They promised to get back to him and, true to their word, he received a phone call the very next day to ask if he would be willing to fly out to Ethiopia to help set up a new hospital that was being built there.

Nick agreed immediately and was told that he'd receive the necessary paperwork in the post. He hung up then sat for a moment, staring at the phone. Before he could go to Ethiopia, he would need to terminate his contract at Dalverston. He didn't think there would be a problem about the hospital releasing him in the circumstances, but there were certain formalities that needed to be completed. Once that was done, he'd be free to go wherever he chose…apart from the one place he longed to be, of course.

His hand shook as he dialled the hospital's number

because it wasn't just a contract he would be breaking but his heart. He really didn't know how he was going to bear being parted from Katie.

Katie had some time owing to her after working over Christmas so took a few days off. She was glad to get away because the strain of pretending that everything was fine was starting to tell on her. There'd still been no word from Nick and each day that had passed seemed to drive another nail through her heart. Mel had recovered from her bout of flu so they spent a day in Manchester but it was less of a break than Katie had hoped it would be. Mel made several references to Nick during the day and Katie had to bite her tongue to stop herself snapping at her friend.

She was glad when they went home and she could be on her own, but once she was back in her room, all she could think about was the time she'd spent there with Nick. In the end, she went to the common room and watched television because it was better than thinking about those few days they'd had together. If it had meant *anything* to Nick he wouldn't have left her, and she had to face that fact, difficult though it was going to be. However, it was when she went into work on the Friday and found a message on her desk, informing her that Dr Lawson had resigned, that everything came to a head. She couldn't believe that Nick had left and that she wouldn't see him again. It didn't seem right and it didn't seem fair. He *owed* her an explanation after what had happened between them!

Picking up the phone, Katie got straight on to the admin department and asked if they had a forwarding address for him. She jotted it down then checked the roster. She was off duty again on Monday so she'd travel down to London then and see Nick. And this time she would make him tell her the truth.

Nick spent the weekend packing so by the time Monday arrived he was all ready to leave. He only had to get himself to the airport but as his flight didn't leave until eight in the evening, he had time to kill first.

He went for a walk and ended up in Regents Park where he had coffee in the café at the zoo. It was a bitterly cold day and he couldn't help thinking about the day he and Katie had spent on Dalverston moor, when they'd stood at the top of that waterfall together. It had been such a magical time that the memory brought a lump to his throat. He realised then that he couldn't leave without telling Katie the truth. Maybe she wouldn't believe him, but he had to try and set the record straight for his own sake at least. He couldn't bear to imagine that Katie thought badly of him.

He went back to the bedsit and settled down to write her a letter, sighing when there was a knock on the door. He really didn't feel like being sociable if one of the other tenants had called round for a chat so he'd get rid of them as fast as possible. He flung open the door and felt all the blood drain from his head when he saw Katie standing outside in the hall.

'Hello, Nick. I'm sorry to barge in like this but I need to talk to you.'

'I...I have to go out,' Nick muttered, so shocked by her arrival that he could barely cobble a sentence together. 'I've a plane to catch and I need to leave for the airport shortly.'

'I'd better keep it brief, then.'

She stalked past him into the room and, short of physically ejecting her, Nick couldn't think of a way to make her leave. He closed the door, desperately trying to curb the overwhelming urge he felt to haul her into his arms as he turned to face her. He couldn't do that because Katie deserved so much more than to have her name linked with a man whose reputation was in tatters.

'I won't beat about the bush, Nick. The reason I've come here today is because I want you to tell me if there was any truth in that story the paper printed.' She looked defiantly at him but he could see the tremor that passed through her body and his heart ached because he knew that he was responsible for causing her all this distress. 'I think you owe me that much, don't you?'

Katie could feel her nerves humming with tension so that it was all she could do to stand there and face him. She'd spent the whole of the train journey working out what she was going to say when she saw Nick and she'd been word-perfect by the time she'd reached London. However, it was one thing to rehearse what she wanted to say and another thing entirely to put it into practice.

'I really can't see the point of this—' he began.

'Well, I can!' She rounded on him as all the pent-up emotions she'd held in check suddenly surfaced. 'How dare you walk out on me like that? Maybe you don't give a damn about me, Nick, but at the very least you could have told me you were leaving!'

'Of course I care about you! Why do you think I left?' He took a couple of quick strides so that, suddenly, he was standing in front of her. 'I didn't want you getting *hurt*, Katie. That's why I left. I didn't want your name being linked with mine because I know the damage it could have caused for you both professionally and personally!'

'Because what that paper printed was true?' she said sickly.

'No! Because the people who *read* it believed that it was true!'

He grasped hold of her arms and she could feel his fingers biting into her flesh. 'It doesn't matter a damn if that story was true or not. I was accused of killing my own brother by driving when I was drunk, and that's the *only* thing that people care about!'

'No, you're wrong because it matters to me, Nick. *I* care if it's true because I care about you.' She reached up and touched his face, feeling the shudder that ran through him, and her heart suddenly overflowed with tenderness. She had no idea if Nick was guilty as charged but it no longer mattered.

She looked deep into his eyes, hoping he could see that she meant every word. 'Don't you understand, Nick? I love you and anything that hurts you hurts me as well.'

'You love me?'

Katie saw the rest of the colour drain from his face and realised that she'd been wrong to blurt it out like that. It certainly wasn't what she'd planned on doing when she'd set off that morning and the thought that she might have embarrassed him was more than she could bear. She pulled away from him and hurried to the door.

'Katie, don't go. I know I've made a complete and total mess of everything but, please, don't leave like this.'

'I shouldn't have come,' she said brokenly. 'If I've embarrassed you, Nick, I'm sorry because I didn't intend to do that.'

'Embarrassed me?' The incredulity in his voice made

her turn and her heart began to race when she saw the expression on his face, all the wonderment that was so clear to see. 'I'm not embarrassed, my love. I'm elated!'

'You are?'

'Uh-huh. And if you come back here I'll show you just how happy I am.'

Katie flushed when he smiled at her because it was such a sensual smile that it sent an immediate wave of desire rushing through her body. She took a hesitant step away from the door then gasped when Nick swiftly covered the rest of the distance that separated them and pulled her into his arms. He kissed her hard and hungrily, leaving her in no doubt whatsoever about his feelings, but obviously he didn't intend there to be any more mistakes.

He drew back and looked into her eyes. 'I love you, too, Katie Denning. I'm absolutely crazy about you, in fact, and these past few weeks apart from you have been a living hell.'

'For me, too,' she admitted shakily. 'I thought you didn't care and that's why you didn't get in touch with me.'

'And I'll never, *ever* forgive myself for that.' He kissed her again with such tenderness this time that tears spilled down her cheeks and she heard him sigh.

'I am *so* sorry, Katie. I never meant to put you through such heartache.'

'I know, and I forgive you. It doesn't matter so long as we can sort this out, and we can, can't we?' she added uncertainly.

Nick pressed another kiss to her mouth then led her to the settee and sat down, drawing her into his arms as though he couldn't bear not to touch her. 'I hope so, but I want you to promise me that you will think about what you're doing and what it could mean for your life if you marry me.'

'Marry you,' she repeated dazedly.

'Of course,' he said with a touch of arrogance. 'I love you and you love me so obviously we're going to get married.'

'I think we should discuss that after we've sorted out all the other issues,' she told him firmly, though her heart was turning cartwheels with joy.

'That sounds ominous but I won't argue with you right now.' He kissed her again then sighed. 'Where shall I start?'

'At the beginning. Tell me what happened to your brother.'

'Yes, you're right. It's time I did that. In fact, I was going to tell you the night before the paper printed that story. I was actually on my way to see you when I was summoned to A and E to deal with a patient.'

'If you were going to tell me then why did you change your mind?'

'Because it just seemed too much to ask of you. I've had to live with this for ten years and I know how damaging it has been. It didn't seem fair to drag you into it.

'It wasn't the first time the press had printed that story, you see. There was a lot of media interest after Mike died so, in a way, I'm not surprised the story surfaced again. The problem was that the reporter didn't check his facts properly. Yes, Mike was killed because the driver of the car he was travelling in was over the limit and, yes, the driver's name was Nicholas Lawson, but it wasn't me. It was my father. He was driving at the time and I blame myself for that.'

'Why?' Katie demanded incredulously. 'How can you be at fault if you weren't driving the car?'

'Because Mike had asked me if I'd pick him up from his friend's house that night and I'd refused. I'd made plans to go to the cinema, you see, so I told Mike that he'd have to get a taxi home and thought no more about it.'

'So what happened? Why did your father go for him?' she prompted when he fell silent. She took hold of his hand and held it tightly because she knew how difficult it must be for him to talk about the tragedy.

'Apparently, Mike phoned up and told Mum that he couldn't get a taxi so she sent Dad to fetch him.' He shrugged. 'What none of us knew at the time was that Dad had started drinking heavily. His business was going through a bad patch and he'd turned to alcohol as a crutch.

'He was well over the limit that night and must have known it, too, but he didn't tell Mum because he didn't want her to know that he had a problem. He picked Mike up but on the way back ran off the road and crashed into a ditch. Mike was killed outright but there wasn't a scratch on Dad, amazingly enough.'

He took a deep breath but Katie could hear the strain in his voice. 'I found them when I was coming home. Dad was just sitting by the car in a daze. I don't think he really knew what had happened. There was nothing I could do for Mike. He was already dead. He was just nineteen at the time, two years younger than me.'

'Oh, Nick, how awful for you!' She wrapped her arms around him and hugged him.

'It was awful. On top of the shock of losing Mike there was all the rest to contend with. Mum blamed Dad for driving when he was drunk and they ended up getting divorced because of it. Somehow or other the papers got the idea that I'd been driving so they printed my details.' He shrugged when she gasped in dismay. 'It was an easy mistake because I was at the hospital with Mike and then I went to the police station afterwards. They probably confused the name and the age of the driver, but a lot of people read the report and believed that I was the guilty party. Then an old girlfriend of Mike's sold some stupid story to the press about me having a history of drinking and driving.

'It was a pack of lies, of course, but everything was such a mess at home, with Mum and Dad rowing, that it didn't seem worth worrying about what the papers were saying. I knew that once the case went to court the truth would come out eventually. Anyway, if I hadn't been so bloody selfish in the first place it would never have happened.'

'That's not true! It wasn't your fault, Nick. You didn't know your father was drinking, let alone that he'd be stupid enough to drive when he was over the limit.'

'Maybe not, but if I'd picked Mike up he'd be here today. He'd be getting on with his life, doing all the things he'd planned…'

His voice broke and he couldn't go on. Katie gathered him close and held him while he cried out his grief and pain. She couldn't begin to imagine how hard it must have been for him these past years, continually blaming himself for his brother's death. Guilt had been eating away at him and she could only hope that it would help to have got it out into the open at last.

He ran his hands over his face and sighed. 'So now you know the whole sorry tale. Not very pretty, is it?'

'No, it's very sad. But you must see that punishing

yourself won't change what's happened. It won't bring your brother back.'

'I know that. I also know now that Mike would hate to think of me being unhappy. He was such a great guy. He was going to change the world and he'd have done it, too.'

'And you've been trying to fulfil his dreams for him?' she suggested softly.

'I've tried. Oh, Mike wasn't interested in medicine. Engineering was his thing and he was particularly interested in working in developing countries. That's one of the reasons why I joined the aid agency because in my own way I felt that I, too, could make a difference...' He broke off and gasped. 'I'm supposed to be on my way to the airport! I've agreed to go on another mission to Ethiopia.'

'Ethiopia?'

'I know, I know. The timing couldn't be worse, could it?' He grinned at her. 'You've just told me that you love me and here I am about to fly to the other side of the world!'

She chuckled. 'It does seem a bit unfortunate.'

'Unfortunate?' Nick rolled his eyes. 'I'm desperate to get you into bed and show you how much I love you and you call it unfortunate.'

'There's a time and a place,' she advised him primly, standing up.

'And this is neither,' he finished for her. He stood up and took her in his arms. 'I love you, Katie. I want to spend my life with you so do you think you could wait for me? I promise to get back to England just as soon as I can. Scout's honour.'

'Oh, I'm not sure about that,' she teased, then gasped

when he kissed her. She was trembling when it ended and Nick looked smugly at her.

'You were saying, sweetheart?'

'You are far too full of yourself, Nick Lawson!'

'But you love me anyway?'

'I suppose so,' she admitted grudgingly.

'That's all I needed to hear.'

One last kiss then he let her go and picked up his bag. 'Fancy a trip to Heathrow? It's a three hour check-in so once I've got rid of my baggage we could find some place to while away the time.'

'What did you have in mind?'

'Well, if my memory serves me correctly there are some rather nice hotels at Heathrow. How do you fancy seeing if there's a room free?'

Katie laughed. 'On one condition.'

'And that is?'

'That we discuss that proposal you intend to make.'

'The one that involves going down on one knee and asking for your hand in marriage?'

'That's the one.'

'Then you have a deal. One proposal coming right up!'

He kissed her again, just briefly but with a wealth of promise, and Katie sighed. They might only have a couple of hours to look forward to at the moment but she intended to make the most of them.

EPILOGUE

THREE months later…

'You look stunning, Katie.'

'Do you think so? Are you sure the dress is all right? I wasn't sure if it was a bit much…'

'It's your wedding day! No bride can be too dressed up on her special day,' Mel said firmly, and Katie laughed.

She smoothed down the skirt of the glorious ivory silk gown and sighed with happiness. Her wedding day promised to be the culmination of three months of pure bliss. Life had been so perfect, in fact, that sometimes she had to pinch herself to prove that she wasn't dreaming.

Nick had spent just a month in Ethiopia before the agency had found a replacement for him. He'd flown home to England and moved straight back to Dalverston and into the flat she'd found for them. He had rescinded his resignation after Niall had offered him his job back once he'd explained what had really happened to his brother.

Nick had also decided to make sure the story would never surface again and had contacted the newspaper and demanded that they print a retraction as well as an apology, which they had done. Everyone had been very supportive since then and a few people had apologised to Nick for ever doubting him. It was all over and done with now and Katie knew that a huge weight had been lifted off his shoulders since he'd shed the burden of guilt that he'd carried for so long.

Life on the maternity unit had gradually settled down although Abbey had decided to leave once she had completed her training. She had taken a job as a community midwife attached to a practice in Cumbria and was slowly getting her life back on track after all the upset. The police had interviewed Gary Hutchins after several people had mentioned seeing him with Abbey at the ball. When a woman living in the same building as Abbey identified Hutchins as the man she'd seen leaving Abbey's flat the day after the ball, the police had authorised DNA tests to be carried out on him. A positive match had been found with one of the samples taken from Abbey so the police had charged him. They had also checked back through their records and discovered a similar incident that had occurred during Hutchins's previous rotation at a different hospital so they were looking into that as well. Hutchins had been suspended until the case came to court and the BMA would review his position after the trial ended.

So much had happened in a few short months, in fact, and so many lives had changed. Now Katie knew that she was about to face the biggest change that had ever happened to her. She took a deep breath before she turned away from the mirror but she didn't have any doubts about what she was doing. She was going to marry Nick that day and she didn't intend to keep him waiting!

'Are we all set?' she demanded, picking up the hand-tied bouquet of lilies of the valley.

'It's tradition for the bride to be late,' Mel pointed out, picking up her own posy of flowers. Katie had been a little bit worried about having to tell Mel about her and Nick, but her friend had taken the news in her stride and had thrown herself into the wedding preparations with great enthusiasm.

'Maybe it is, but this particular bride intends to be right on time,' Katie told her firmly, opening the front door. She'd decided not to have anyone give her away on the day so she and Mel travelled together in the limousine that Nick had insisted on ordering for her. The wedding was being held in the hospital's chapel and it looked as though every member of staff who wasn't on duty that day had turned up to witness the marriage when they arrived.

Katie had eyes for only one person, however, the most important person in her life. Nick was standing beside the front pew and the expression on his face as she walked down the aisle towards him filled her with joy. He took her hands and bent to kiss her when she reached him.

'I love you, Katie Denning,' he whispered, before he led her to the altar where the minister was waiting.

Katie clung to his hand as they repeated their vows in front of all their friends. She meant every word and knew that Nick meant them, too. When the minister declared them to be man and wife, a great cheer erupted as Nick swept her into his arms. Katie smiled up at him, all the love she felt clear to see in her eyes. This was a new beginning for both of them, their future to be spent loving and caring for one another, and she could hardly wait for the next phase of her life to begin.

'I love you, too, Nick. Now, always—'

'And for ever,' he finished for her, then kissed her, putting the final seal on all the promises they'd made.

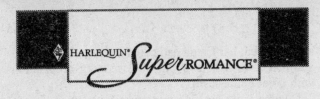

...there's more to the story!

Superromance.
A *big* satisfying read about unforgettable characters. Each month we offer *six* very different stories that range from family drama to adventure and mystery, from highly emotional stories to romantic comedies—and much more! Stories about people you'll believe in and care about. Stories too compelling to put down....

Our authors are among today's *best* romance writers. You'll find familiar names and talented newcomers. Many of them are award winners— and you'll see why!

If you want the biggest and best in romance fiction, you'll get it from Superromance!

Emotional, Exciting, Unexpected...

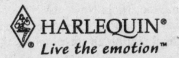

HARLEQUIN®
Live the emotion™

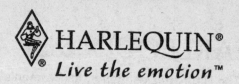
HARLEQUIN®
Live the emotion™

 HARLEQUIN®
 AMERICAN *Romance*®

Upbeat,
All-American Romances

 HARLEQUIN®
 flipside

Romantic Comedy

Harlequin Historicals®

Historical,
Romantic Adventure

HARLEQUIN®
INTRIGUE

Romantic Suspense

HARLEQUIN®
 HARLEQUIN ROMANCE®

The essence of
modern romance

HARLEQUIN®
 *Presents*

Seduction and passion
guaranteed

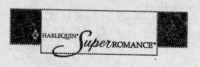 HARLEQUIN® Super*ROMANCE*®

Emotional,
Exciting, Unexpected

 *Temptation*

Sassy, Sexy, Seductive!

eHARLEQUIN.com

The Ultimate Destination for Women's Fiction

For FREE online reading, visit
www.eHarlequin.com now and enjoy:

Online Reads
Read **Daily** and **Weekly** chapters from
our Internet-exclusive stories by your
favorite authors.

Interactive Novels
Cast your vote to help decide how these
stories unfold...then stay tuned!

Quick Reads
For shorter romantic reads, try our
collection of Poems, Toasts, & More!

Online Read Library
Miss one of our online reads?
Come here to catch up!

Reading Groups
Discuss, share and rave with other
community members!

For great reading online,
visit www.eHarlequin.com today!

INTONL04R

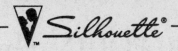

Emotional, compelling stories that capture the intensity of living, loving and creating a family in today's world.

Modern, passionate reads that are powerful and provocative.

Romances that are sparked by danger and fueled by passion.

SILHOUETTE *Romance*

From today to forever, these love stories offer today's woman fairytale romance.

Action-filled romances with strong, sexy, savvy women who save the day.

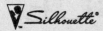

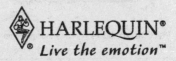